STO

DO NOT REMOVE
CARDS FROM POCKET

2/92

LESSONS IN FEAR

A Carter Colborn Mystery

by
DIANA SHAW

Troll Associates

A TROLL BOOK, published by Troll Associates,
Mahwah, NJ 07430

Published by arrangement with Little Brown and Company, Inc.
For information address Little Brown and Company, Inc.,
34 Beacon Street, Boston, Massachusetts, 02108.

First Troll Printing, 1988

Printed in the United States of America.

10 9 8 7 6 5 4 3 2 1

ISBN 0-8167-1315-4

For
Carol C.,
the Original

CHAPTER 1

I felt three taps on my chair, and slid my hand behind my back so Linsey could slip her note into it.

"Ms. Colborn!" Balboa's voice hit me like a slap. "Do you want me to read it, or will you share it with the rest of us?"

I looked at the paper that'd been passed to me and saw that the note couldn't be read. It could barely even be described. The only way to share it would be to pass it around, which wouldn't have been a good idea, considering what it was: a drawing of Balboa, and not a very flattering one.

Linsey had exaggerated her bulging eyes so they hung out of their sockets, and had made her bowed legs into a perfect zero. She didn't need to exaggerate the expression: Balboa always looked like we were an irritating TV show and she was about to turn off the set.

She'd drawn her hair pretty much the way it was — a mess — adding a rodent whose tail went in one ear and came out to curl around the other. In the picture, Balboa was about to bite into a sandwich that was clearly a dead frog between two slices of bread. You didn't have to guess where Linsey got the inspiration for that: the day before, someone had dropped a frog left over from dissection into Balboa's lunch bag. Probably Judy Mancini or Corey Phipps. They believe in animal rights, including the right not to be pinned to a board and sliced open by ninth graders.

"Well?" Balboa was waiting for me to decide.

"I'll read it," I said, clearing my throat to give my imagination the time it needed for this job.

Some people say my imagination works overtime. Right then I wished it was true. My mother, for one, says it, especially whenever I'm on a case. That's because she doesn't approve of my detective work. Even when I have the most convincing clues, suspects, and evidence in the world, she'll say it's all in my head.

"The note says, 'I have terrible laryngitis, so if Mrs. Balboa calls on me, please explain that I will write my answer instead of saying it.'"

Linsey was so surprised, she laughed — loud and clear. While I turned the note into confetti, Mrs. Balboa gave us each a ticket to detention.

I looked around for sympathy and found Neil smiling some my way. Neil is in love with me, which can be a pain. I like hanging out with him, but it's not true love. He's got a good sense of humor — he draws cartoons for the school paper — and he's a good friend; you can tell him things like how much you hate it at home after your parents' divorce without him blabbing it all over town. He's also a walking library — full of plots and facts from the books and magazines he's always reading.

But he's not my type. My type would be taller than me, his shoulders would be broad enough to fit into a leather jacket, he'd have piercing green eyes, and he'd play lacrosse. In fact, he'd be exactly like Tony Von Thelan, who I've been in love with since fifth grade, but who still hasn't noticed me, or at least not in the way I mean. Tony's what you'd call a hunk and a half.

Neil is shorter than me, and I'm probably the shortest girl in the ninth grade. He's skinny and he's got black eyes that are all cloudy under these thick glasses he has to wear.

Balboa noticed where Neil was looking, and waved a detention slip in his face. He straightened up, fast. It was one thing to feel sorry for me, and another to want to keep me company. Detention with Balboa is not something you would do if you could avoid it. Once she made Cheryl Sykes clean up after the tenth graders dissected fetal pigs. Cheryl had to do it bare-handed — picking up their gutted little bodies and chucking them into a Hefty bag. I heard she smelled so bad her boyfriend, Owen, wouldn't kiss her for two weeks.

That's the kind of thing that made Balboa the

most unpopular teacher at Thomas A. Dooley High School ("TAD" for short). I only knew one person who actually liked Balboa and that, believe it or not, was my own brother, Justin. I can't explain it except that Justin is really into science, and I guess she liked having a student who took her seriously. Everyone else was just trying to pass, and for them it was cool to make fun of Balboa, even about things that normally you wouldn't joke about. Like how she got her limp.

The story was that it happened when Balboa was hiking and a rattlesnake bit her on the ankle. She cut a hunk of skin out from around the bite and sucked the poison out. By the time she got to a doctor it was too late to close up the hole, so she had to get a brace that made her limp.

The end of the story is that Balboa survived the snakebite, but, after one taste of Balboa, the snake died.

It makes sense that since practically none of the students liked Balboa, the parents and the school board thought she was great. TAD needed a new principal and a lot of parents wanted Balboa for the job because she was famous for all the stuff they thought TAD was missing, like discipline and "high academic standards" (meaning stiff grading). It was true that things were pretty slack at TAD. Most of the teachers would give you an A just to keep you and your parents from hassling them.

Balboa was not like that. When she gave you a grade, she meant it. And if you failed a test, she didn't let you keep taking it until you passed or let you make up for it with an extra-credit project.

Merry didn't seem too concerned about whether Balboa caught her or not. She smiled at me, and shrugged, like she was saying, "I guess there's nothing you can do." Merry Jordan's my best friend, which you might think is strange if you knew how little we have in common. For one thing, Merry is always looking for the best side of people, while I've made something of a hobby out of suspecting everyone of the worst.

Not that I was paying much attention in the first place, but after that, I *really* couldn't concentrate on the lesson — a review for the big test that was coming up. I spent the rest of class worrying about my future, which was now in doubt thanks to the detention slip.

My mother had sworn she'd send me to boarding school next year if my discipline record didn't improve by the end of this one. Not that I would mind being away from my mother, but the thought of *living* at school and the idea of leaving my friends were too much.

It was almost the end of the year and I could make wallpaper from the detention slips I'd gotten so far. I don't go looking for trouble; I seem to be able to find it without making any effort at all. I don't even remember what all the detentions were for — mostly correcting the teacher (they call it "talking back"), or reading *Armchair Detective* magazine in class.

This detention also meant I'd miss the newspaper meeting that afternoon. And that meant I'd be stuck with the assignments nobody else wanted, like covering the yearbook committee meeting or the history club's field trip to Fort Ticonderoga.

I wouldn't mind making those sacrifices for a friend. But it wasn't worth it for Linsey, who I didn't know very well. She was a junior, but was taking my biology class because the school she'd gone to before this year didn't have ninth-grade biology, which you need to graduate from TAD. She's one of those people who act like they don't study or care but she actually does both, and has the grades to prove it.

"Good luck," Neil said to me after class. "I don't mean to scare you or anything" — he smiled his halfway grin — "but I heard that the last students she held for detention had to be locked up in Western State. She drove them craaazy." He crossed his eyes and wagged his tongue.

"It probably won't be that bad," Merry said. "Not any worse than having an extra class period with her."

"That's bad enough," I said.

"Come on, you guys. I don't think she's that bad," Merry insisted.

Neil and I gave her a where-have-you-been-all-year look. But that's Merry.

"You're right, Merry," I said. "Having class with Balboa is my second-favorite thing. My first favorite is chewing on glass."

"Well," Neil said as I headed off for gym class,

"maybe you'll break your leg or crack your head open in gym. Then you'd get out of detention."

"Thanks," I said. "I'll do my best."

"Have you voted yet?"

It was election day at TAD, and the frizzy blonde with the pink turtleneck, big legs, and bouquet of baby roses wanted me to vote for her.

"I . . . no," I said. She gave me a rose, and smiled so I couldn't help smiling back.

"I'm Adrian, and I'd appreciate your vote. I have to get to class, but ask any of my campaign helpers, and they'll tell you what I'll do if I get elected."

She didn't have to tell me who she was. She was Adrian Attridge. And I felt bad standing there smiling and taking her rose because the thing is, I couldn't stand Adrian Attridge. True, I didn't even know her; I had never talked to her; but still, I couldn't stand her.

I had my reasons. Maybe it was only one reason. But one *good* reason: *everyone* liked her.

Honor roll, pep squad, district debating champion, president of the drama club — she seemed to get everything she aimed for. If she were better looking, she'd have it all. But "cute" was about as far as you could stretch it with Adrian. You'd think that more people would be like me and hate her for being so popular. But she had more friends than I'll have in my whole life, more than I'd even have time to talk to. Everyone admired the way she juggled her social life with doing well in school. They said she was good without being a goody-goody.

She was running to be head of the Ambassadors, four seniors who are supposed to promote school spirit and give the school a good image in the community. They supervise the hall monitors and the litter patrol. Plus they do volunteer work in town, like at a hospital or nursing home, so everyone in St. Davids will think that all TAD students are that good. Ha.

At the end of each year, before the old Ambassadors graduate, the school votes for a new head Ambassador. Then the head Ambassador gets to pick the other three.

One thing I'll say for Adrian, she was the only candidate to bother with the ninth graders. The rest ignored us like they didn't expect us to care enough about the school to vote. At least she was showing us some respect.

"They're going to close the ballot box next period," she said, moving ahead into Balboa's advanced biology class. "It's in the cafeteria."

I was halfway down the hall, thinking that I'd probably been unfair to Adrian and maybe I *should* vote for her, when I realized I'd left my knapsack in Balboa's room. When I got back there, Adrian had stuck her flowers into a big glass jar and was trying to give them to Balboa.

"I'd prefer getting an A paper from you, or at least one that would indicate you care about what goes on in this class," Balboa said. Adrian went red.

A few people giggled, but only a few. Adrian was popular, Balboa was not.

I got my bag and bolted. The bell was going to ring any minute, and all I needed was another detention slip, for being late.

I wasn't about to face Balboa alone, so when school got out I hung around outside the classroom until Linsey arrived, pissed off about having to miss play practice. (The drama club was doing *Guys and Dolls*, and she was designing the sets.) We wished each other good luck and went in. But Balboa wasn't there. "Maybe she forgot — let's go," Linsey said.

"Balboa forget? Be serious."

"You're right." We were scanning the room when Linsey's face froze, her eyes going wider until the brows nearly ended up on top of her head. I followed her gaze to the storage closet, where I saw a pair of red tennis shoes sticking out into the classroom. A pair of legs were attached to them, and the rest of Balboa followed.

CHAPTER 2

"Oh my God, Mrs. Balboa, are you all right?" Linsey squatted beside the teacher. "What happened?"

But Balboa wasn't talking; she was out. Cold.

I checked to see if she was breathing, and was grateful to find that she was. I admit it wasn't the kind of thing to be thinking at a time like this, but the last thing I wanted was to have to give her mouth-to-mouth.

Linsey was getting up, or at least trying to, but her feet started sliding around like she was totally uncoordinated. Finally she went down, butt first. "*Shit!*" she said, covering her mouth as if Balboa might have heard.

I reached to help her up, but my feet started to go ahead of me. I grabbed a shelf to keep from sliding further. Linsey would have to get up on her own, which, after sliding around awhile, she finally did. Then she left to get Musgrove, the vice principal, who was acting principal for the moment, since Mr. Massey had just left for another school.

I made my way around the closet to see if I could find out where the slippery stuff had come from, and what it was. Where it was coming from was a plastic jar that had turned on its side. What it was, was a clear liquid with no smell and no label.

It looked like Balboa had had an accident, which was too bad in a way because it would've been more interesting to discover, for example, that someone had tripped her or pushed her. Not that I wished something like that had happened to her — I was angry at her for the detention, but still, I wouldn't wish that on her. It's just that I hadn't had a case in a while, and I was getting bored, and rusty.

Gripping the shelf and watching my feet, I carried the jar out of the closet, put the lid on it, and dropped it into my knapsack. Merry, the science brain, would be able to tell me what it was.

Musgrove arrived, shedding sweat as if he'd run the marathon instead of the one flight of stairs from his office. Everyone calls him "Moosegrove" because of the way he's built. You could fit four or five of my father into one of his suits, and still the shoulder seams wouldn't strain the way they do when Musgrove squeezes into them. His face looks like it was carved from a block of melting ice; instead of having cheekbones and a chin, everything from his forehead to his neck runs together.

Linsey warned him about the floor, so he held on to the shelf while he knelt to feel Balboa's pulse.

"How long has she been like this?" Musgrove was talking to me. "What happened?"

"I don't know," I said. "It looks like she slipped on the floor."

I felt bad for Musgrove. It was obvious he didn't have a clue what to do. Musgrove can be really out of it, like when he called a special assembly to talk about the dangers of listening to rock music. First of all, the records he played were at least two years old, so he was telling us we shouldn't listen to albums that nobody *would* listen to, anyway. And second, no one takes it as seriously as he thinks we do. We either like a song or we don't. Nobody is going to burn down the school just because Search and Destroy has a song about it.

The rescue-squad siren began as a whine way in the distance and got louder and louder until it reached the school door, where it croaked and died. Musgrove's face became a normal color again once he realized he wouldn't have to take care of Balboa anymore.

"I guess there's no point in being here if she's not here," Linsey said. "I'm going to play practice."

"And I'm going to the newspaper." Did I have a story!

I could hear the editor's voice as I got closer to the room where we held our meetings. "We need a story about replacing Mr. Massey with a new principal. Who wants to do it?" I stopped dead. It was one of the last things I wanted to write about, and going in then might have given Sheila, the editor, ideas.

"My mother's on the school board," I heard Wayne Davis say. "I can do it." I walked on in. "I'll tell you one thing I know," Wayne continued. "It's between Musgrove and Balboa." Everyone groaned.

Neil was surprised to see me. "How did you get out?"

"You won't believe it. Just wait." I took the seat next to him.

"Carter, I'm glad you could make it." Sheila was being sarcastic. "You didn't by any chance happen to bring that story?"

I hadn't. I hadn't even *started* it. But I didn't tell her that. I didn't have to. She knew.

"Carter, I want that story. I needed it a week ago. What's the problem?"

I had been assigned a story on the new fire-drill procedures. The problem was that it's not one of those assignments that make you jump out of bed in the morning feeling glad to be alive. But that's not what I said. "The fire commissioner's line was busy every time I tried it." This actually was true, even if I'd tried his line only once.

"Anyway," I said, changing the subject, "I've got another story. They just carted Balboa off to the hospital. I found her. She fell and went unconscious."

"You sure she's not dead?" Stephen Sylvester asked. He was being sarcastic, too.

"Was she really unconscious?" someone else wanted to know. "How could you tell?"

I could understand their attitude. I had pretty much of a reputation for exaggerating things. It had gotten the paper into trouble once or maybe twice, but that's another story. I ignored them and waited to hear what Sheila would say.

But before Sheila could say anything, Barb Mantell came in to tell us that Adrian Attridge had won the election and would be the new head Ambassador. From the reactions in the room, you could tell that almost everyone had voted for her. Barb left and Sheila got back to me. "That's yours, too," she said, reminding me that at the last meeting she'd told me to cover the Ambassador election and interview the winner.

"Okay, I'll do the Ambassador story, I promise, by tomorrow. Just let me write up the Balboa thing, too."

"The fire drill . . ."

"Okay, I'll do that, too."

"And I still need someone to cover the history club field trip . . ."

"Okay, I'll do that, too." I would have volunteered for every assignment for the whole paper if she'd let me write up what I'd seen that afternoon.

"You're crazy, Carter. You barely make your deadlines when I give you one story. You never make them when I give you two. And now you want four?"

"You'll see."

"Okay." She gave in, but she didn't like it. "Have those stories the day after tomorrow. No later."

It was a little after four, and I knew where to find Adrian. On my way, I stopped in the bathroom to make sure I didn't have any leftover lunch on my face or anything like that.

I've heard different things about the way I look. Some people say I'm "exotic," which is just another word for weird. My father and Justin say I'm pretty — but what else are they going to say? Relatives don't count when it comes to your looks.

One thing that makes me "exotic," I guess, is my skin color, which is dark for someone with sandy hair like mine. Whenever someone talks about a beautiful blonde, they usually say she has a "peaches and cream" complexion. My mother took me to a beauty consultant once, and she said you'd call my skin color "olive." It's not green or anything. It's just called that. Seriously.

Another thing is that my nose turns up a little. Justin says it means I'm a born snob. I've been trying to think of something to say back to him, but the truth is, he's too good-looking.

My eyes are perfectly round; "as big as quarters" is what Merry says. Brown. They make me look innocent. I'd give anything for eyes like my mother's, which are green and shaped like a cat's. They make her look mysterious and slightly evil.

What I like most about me is the way I'm built. I'm "compact" and I've got killer muscles from riding my bike. Whenever I'm bored, I tense my calves and watch them bulge out.

I assumed the singing I heard as I got closer to the auditorium was coming from a record. But when I slipped through the door, I saw that it was coming from Adrian Attridge. She was singing a song about being a bell that was ringing. The song sounded silly, but she was good. She was *very* good, so I couldn't understand why she stopped herself halfway through and said, "I'll *never* get it."

"Sounded great to me," Josh Dickerson called from the wall where he was working the stage lights.

"Yeah, Adri, it was great," Linsey said from offstage.

"But . . ." Adrian started to explain what she thought was wrong, then shrugged. "Okay, I'll try it again."

And she did, sounding no different — just as good as she did before. When she stopped this time, it wasn't because she didn't like the way she sounded. It was because of me.

"I'm sorry, rehearsals are for drama club only," she said.

"I just wanted to know when I could interview you for the *TAD Times*."

"I already told someone from the paper I don't want anything written about the show until we open." She winked, knelt, and knocked on the wood floor. "Bad luck."

"It's not about the show. It's about the Ambassadors."

She smiled the way she had when she'd handed me the rose — so I couldn't help smiling back. "Great. Anytime . . . except right now, of course."

"Okay, then, when?"

"Six o'clock? My house? Four-two-two-one Arbordale? Okay?"

"Okay. Thanks."

"Thank *you*." Adrian didn't start her song again until I had left the auditorium and gone halfway down the hall.

CHAPTER 3

Adrian's house was pretty much the same as most other houses in St. Davids, Pennsylvania, including mine. What made our houses different, besides the fact that hers was yellow and mine was white, was that both of her parents still lived at hers. My dad lives in Los Angeles now. He moved there a few months ago, after the divorce.

Mrs. Attridge came to the door wearing a smile and an apron, reminding me of the mothers you see on TV shows about happy families. "Adrian told me you were coming." She led me down a hall, carpeted in red. The walls inside were yellow, too, and one of them was covered with pictures of Adrian — a history of her life in pictures.

"You're doing a story about her for the paper," Mrs. Attridge said. "I think that's wonderful. Did you see the one about her in the *St. Davids Tribune*?"

"I must have missed it," I said, smiling to be polite.

"Here." She pointed to one of the frames on the wall. In it was a newspaper clipping — the headline DEBATE CHAMP over a short article and a photograph of Adrian holding a trophy. It was the kind of article that ran about Adrian in the local paper every few weeks, and made parents all over town ask their kids why they couldn't be more like her.

"This one is my favorite," Mrs. Attridge said, pointing to a picture of Adrian at age two or three, wearing a sweatshirt that said HARVARD CLASS OF ????. "Her father and I have always known Adrian would do well . . . even if we've had to push her every once in a while.

"You know Adrian is the star of *Guys and Dolls*," Mrs. Attridge went on.

"I know. I heard her sing today."

She leaned toward me. "This might be cute in your article. . . . When she was a little girl, Adrian was so shy about performing in front of strangers, she would stop singing if an airplane flew overhead . . . she was afraid the passengers might hear her!"

I was beginning to wonder how anyone could've survived sixteen years with that woman when Adrian, the survivor, called from the next room, "Mother, Carter doesn't want to hear about my childhood. Please send her in."

Mrs. Attridge leaned toward me again. "Sometimes she can be such a boss." She seemed proud of it, though, and pointed me toward the study.

Adrian was curled in a chair with a book. She raised one index finger at me, meaning "one second." I sat down and fumbled with my notepad, pretending to go over the questions I was going to ask her.

"It's great. You've got to read it," she said, reaching to put the book into my lap. I looked at the title: *Nutcracker*.

"It's about this woman who gets her son to kill her father so she can inherit his money. The best thing is that it's true. I know it sounds trashy, but the author is a famous journalist who writes really well. Take it. You especially would like it, since you're a journalist."

I blushed when she referred to me "especially." I didn't think the most popular girl in school had given any thought to me.

"And you're the best, too. Your stories are the liveliest, even if I'm not always sure you're not exaggerating a little." She smiled with the corner of her mouth. Before I could unknot my tongue to thank her, she went on, "The way you described the cafeteria when we decorated it for homecoming . . ."

Again my face changed color — she and the other members of the homecoming court had spent days doing the decorations and what I'd written wasn't the most flattering thing you've ever read.

"Don't worry about it," she said. "I know it looked like 'a gorilla went berserk in a party supply shop.'" Those were the exact words I'd used.

What could I say to that? She spared me by

changing the subject. "So," she said, "you want to know how I feel about being head Ambassador."

"That's right," I said.

"It's great." She noticed I didn't write anything down. "I know that doesn't give you a whole lot to put in your story, but that's the answer: it feels great."

Even though she seemed to have finished, I didn't say anything. It's an interview technique I learned from Art, my dad. If you wait long enough after a question, you'll get a much better answer than the one that comes out first.

"I'm used to getting awards and things from teachers and adults," she said, proving my point, "but to get an honor like this from the other kids at school . . . it's really special."

I wrote that down.

"Carter?" I looked up from my pad. "Do you mind not putting that in your story? It sounds kind of snotty, and I don't want to come off that way."

"It sounds fine," I said. "But if you really think . . ."

"Thanks."

I went on to the next question. "Why do you think you won?"

"For two reasons. First, I think people liked my ideas."

"For example?"

"During my campaign I kept saying how students and teachers haven't been getting along at TAD, and how I thought something should be done about it. I guess that meant something to everyone, so they voted for me."

"What's the other reason? You said there were two."

"It's that I've proven I'm a good leader."

"How?"

"Just things I've done," she said, looking down.

"Like what?"

"Like, I'm president of the drama club . . ."

"And . . ."

"And head of the pep squad . . ."

"And?"

"And debate squad captain and chairman of the homecoming committee."

She didn't look at me once while she listed her achievements. If I had done all those things, I'd blare it all over town. But she seemed almost embarrassed by them.

"Do you think you'll have any trouble finding three juniors to be the other Ambassadors?"

"The only hard thing will be narrowing it down. There are a lot of really good people in my class."

She leaned toward me like she was going to say my slip was showing. "This is off the record, but *some* people have spent their whole time at TAD trying to become Ambassadors. They've got perfect grades and good extracurricular activities. But I probably won't pick any of them, because I'm going to be considering *character*, and if you spend all your time aiming at one goal, you don't always have time to do the things that make you a good all-around person."

"Why do they want to be Ambassadors so badly?"

"Because it looks good on your college application, and those people think, 'What's the point of going to high school if you're not going to get into a good college?' I think they're missing out on a lot by being so single-minded."

"My brother's an Ambassador —"

She cut in, smiling, "I know."

"And he said it's a tradition for the Ambassadors to have some crazy initiation rites. Like he had to have his legs signed by every girl in his English class. Are you going to do stuff like that?"

"It's a tradition," she said. "So, of course."

"Can you tell me what they're going to be?"

She shook her head.

"Even off the record?"

"Sorry."

"Okay . . . then let me ask you about another tradition. In other years, the person who won the election for head Ambassador has picked the person who lost the election to be one of the Ambassadors. Are you going to do that?"

She leaned toward me again. "No. And if you promise not to say anything, I'll tell you why."

I nodded.

"To be a good Ambassador, you have to be really popular. She lost by too much. . . . If the election had been closer, then I probably would pick her, but . . ." She shook her head, then she sat back. "I know that sounds awful."

I agreed it *sounded* pretty rude. But it made sense, and it was good she was honest about it.

"Just a second," she said, getting up. While she was gone I flipped through *Nutcracker*. Adrian had written her name on the inside, in that curlicue kind of script that the girls in my sixth-grade class used to practice during recess and lunch. I thought it was a waste of time back then, but seeing how clean and lively it looked on the page I wished I had worked harder at it instead of ending up with a signature that looks like a dirty snail has crawled across the paper.

When Adrian came back she was carrying a pouch full of makeup. "I've been looking at you and your great coloring, and thinking I have some stuff that might be right for you."

"Okay," I said, although I didn't know what anyone could do with my looks.

She worked on my face for a few minutes, giving me tips as she went along. "You should be playing up your eyes," she said, coloring them with liner, mascara, and shadow. "The right color lipstick will set them off. . . . Let's try this." She held my chin with one hand, and ran a lipstick over my mouth with the other. Then she handed me a mirror. "What do you think?" she said.

Beautiful would have been an exaggeration, but I looked good. Maybe even very good.

I tried to thank her, but she cut it short and gave me the makeup pouch. "Keep it."

"Are you sure?"

"None of it's right for me. And besides," she said, walking me toward the door, "I want to ask you a favor."

"Sure," I said. Anything.

"Your brother, Justin — he's planning to be premed at college next year?"

"That's what he goes around saying."

"He's really shy, isn't he? I see him at school, but he doesn't seem to have a girlfriend . . ."

"You want to know if he has one."

"Off the record, of course."

"Of course." Justin would flip. Adrian Attridge was interested in him. "No, he doesn't have a girl-friend, not anymore. He used to go with Holly Lasousa, but . . ." I decided not to tell her why they broke up, in case it gave Adrian the wrong idea. Holly dumped Justin because he was too wrapped up in biology. Holly even told him he should be dating Mrs. Balboa, which I think was pretty nasty and unnecessary.

"That's all I wanted to know," she said. "Let me know if you need anything else for your piece."

We smiled at each other. With all the secrets we'd shared, I felt like we were old friends.

CHAPTER 4

"Justin?" Mom heard the door slam and called from somewhere inside the house.

"No. It's only me," I said.

I said "only" because I knew she would have preferred it to be Justin, who, as she reminded me practically every day, was always "helpful and good." As opposed to me, who was "difficult and uncooperative."

Justin doesn't have the trouble with his reputation that I do. Everyone thinks he's great, including my friends, who half the time come over to my house more to see him than to hang out with me.

Mom was in the kitchen, standing in front of an open cabinet with a pad of paper and a pen, eyeing the shelves like a stockboy in the supermarket. She was wearing her white jumpsuit that looks like a karate outfit and her hair was braided and twisted into a bun at the back of her head. We are about the same size, and if you really want to make her happy, ask her if we're sisters.

"Olives, olives, olives . . ." she was muttering, scanning the cans on the shelf. "Do you see any olives up there, Carter?"

"Nope."

"I guess we get olives, then," she said, making a note on the pad. "Any idea what's happened to your brother? I need him to go get some things for me."

"But I thought the party isn't until Saturday night." It was only Tuesday.

"It's not. But it takes an age to get this house ready." She closed the cabinet. "One of these days we're going to move to a tent. And we're not giving out our address to anyone."

I don't know why she kept having parties when all she ever did was complain about them — first about how hard it was to get the house ready, then about how dull everyone was she'd invited, then about how much trouble it was to clean up afterward. But she had them all the time now that Art was gone. I probably wouldn't know I was home if there wasn't a party going on or about to go on. Neil once said it reminded him of this character in a book he'd read — this guy threw huge parties all the time hoping the woman he was in love with would show at one of them. She finally did, but the guy ended up dying pretty soon after that, so what was the point?

If Mom was waiting for the man of her dreams

to show up, she was definitely inviting the wrong people. No one but stiffs — lawyers and stuff. No one fun, like Art.

The front door slammed. "Justin?"

This time she was right.

He came into the kitchen, carrying his books. Some people say Justin and I look alike, which I take as a compliment (unless of course they mean I look like a seventeen-year-old boy, in which case I guess it's not so flattering). But we do have the same shape eyes, the same sandy hair, and the same "olive" skin — only on boys they call it "bronze."

I might have moved to California with Art if it hadn't been for Justin. But would it have been fair to be sunbathing and eating humongous, pulpy oranges in February while he was bundled to the teeth, shoveling the sidewalks for Mom? After everything Justin's done for me — he taught me to ride a bike, he's taken me to movies and concerts when most brothers would rather die than be seen with their sister, and he's covered up for me when I've faked being sick to get out of school — I couldn't do that to him.

"What took you?" I asked. Usually he beats me home from school by a long shot.

"I heard about Mrs. Balboa and stopped at the hospital to see how she was." Mom didn't know about the accident so we filled her in.

"I was there," I said. "I found her."

"So, how is she?" Mom asked.

"Still pretty confused," Justin said. "She's had a concussion."

Justin went to the refrigerator, took out the milk, threw back his head, and drank straight from the carton. If I had done that, Mom would be all over me with a lecture about communicable disease. But he stood there guzzling away.

I was hungry, too. But I knew better than to ask Mom about dinner. After Art left Mom didn't seem to have time to cook. Since then Justin and I had gotten really good at phoning out for pizza, heating up Lean Cuisines, and making spaghetti with sauce from a jar. Some nights we'd just have cereal or sandwiches. This was going to be one of them.

"Think Balboa will be back in school tomorrow?" I asked.

"Probably. You know how she is. She doesn't like to let things get to her," he said, wiping his milk mustache away with the back of his wrist.

"In other words," Mom said, "she's got spirit."

"In other words," I said, "she's stubborn."

"That's a pretty rude thing to say, after what's happened to her," Justin said. I felt guilty, but would never admit it.

Mom tore the list off her pad and held it out for Justin. "Here are a few things I'd like you to get for me."

"Like how soon?"

"Like whenever you get around to it . . . as long as you get around to it by ten tonight."

Justin looked over the list while Mom left to get money for him.

That was my chance.

"Adrian Attridge likes you," I said.

"Yeah? So does the President, the First Lady, and the entire Royal Family."

Before I could start in with some real teasing, Mom came back.

"Speaking of being late" — Mom has this way of switching back to a conversation you thought was over hours ago — "*you* usually get home sooner than this, Carter."

"I had to do an interview for *TAD Times*. With Adrian Attridge, who is in *love* with Justin, only he's pretending not to care."

Justin gave me his would-you-just-cut-that-out look.

"Maybe he *doesn't* care," Mom said. "Just because *you're* boy crazy, don't think everyone spends all their time thinking about the opposite sex."

"I am not boy crazy," I said, when what I should have said was, "Look who's talking." She's the one going out with a new guy every week.

Mom shrugged and poked Justin, handing him a wad of bills.

I left the kitchen to put my books away and when I came back to make my sandwich, Justin was on the phone. The way he looked at me, you'd think I'd caught him in his underwear — or, worse, without it.

"This is Justin Colborn. I'm calling to congratulate you on winning the election."

I'd caught him calling Adrian.

I smiled, put both hands over my heart, and puckered my lips. He turned to face the wall.

"You'll have fun," he said. "Yeah, it is a lot of responsibility, but it's mostly fun. Besides, you're lucky. Being the head, you don't have to do any of the initiation rites. You just get to think them up."

Then he listened for a while. Finally he said, "I'll be glad to. No, seriously, I would. Tomorrow night. Seven thirty? Okay. Great. See ya. And congratulations again."

"What was that all about?" I asked, batting my eyes and sticking my face close to his.

"Adrian wants me to help her with her biology project."

"Yeah. I've heard that one before," I said. "You'll be over there explaining photosynthesis, then *blam* — she'll be running her fingers through your hair and whispering 'Te amo' in your ear."

"I guess you know all this from experience."

"Of course! Why else do guys rampage through here every night to help me with my homework?"

"Anyway, she said to tell you she's decided on one Ambassador: Bob Earle."

Bob Earle was a stringy guy who'd only been at TAD one year after moving up from Maryland. Adrian must have liked the fact that he was new; he hadn't spent his whole high school life trying to become an Ambassador. Bob got straight A's and wanted to go to Princeton, like his father. I don't usually know much about juniors, but I knew about him because Merry had a crush on him, and sent me out to investigate. He was a do-gooder type, so he fit in with what Adrian said about character. Once I was taking the bus to school because it was raining too hard to ride my bike. The bus broke down, and Bob went out in the downpour to look at the engine while the driver called a repair truck. Bob toyed around with it awhile, and we were at school before the repair truck showed.

I had enough to write my story, and after slapping my sandwich together, that's how I spent that night.

Merry's bus was pulling up just as I got to school the next day, so I sped across the parking lot to meet it. I meant to give her the jar of slippery stuff. If she could tell me what it was, I could finish my piece about Balboa and hand it in that afternoon.

That's what I *meant* to do. Instead, I hit a bump, flew over my handlebars, and skidded across the asphalt.

I was more stunned than hurt. I was even *more* stunned — as well as embarrassed beyond belief — when I saw that I hadn't hit a bump, but a pair of legs. Not just any legs, either: when they slithered from underneath the car they were sticking out of, I saw they were Tony Von Thelan's. Peter Findlay came around from the hood and stared at me like he'd never seen anything so dumb in his life.

Tony got up and they both leaned over me, each bent with his hands on his knees and no intention of helping me up. Not because they were mean or rude — it's just the way they were together.

And together is what Findlay and Von Thelan *always* were. No one even bothered to say their names separately; they were called Von Findlay. Their hobbies were cars and lacrosse. Their *lives* were cars and lacrosse — *other* people's cars, since they didn't have their licenses yet, and could only fool around with them, not drive them.

"Are you okay?" Tony's face was so close I could have kissed him without moving anything but my lips. I looked into his eyes for signs of desperate concern. Instead, I saw the reflection of a stupid blonde flat on her ass in the school parking lot.

"Are you okay?" Tony asked again.

"Oh yeah, sure. This happens all the time. I'm training to be a bicycle acrobat. Some days are better than others." I should have just admitted I was uncoordinated and a jerk instead of making things worse by trying to be funny.

"You ran right over his legs," Findlay said, like he was trying to make sense of it.

"I know. I guess I should've been watching for them. It's just that I ride over this spot every day and they've never been here before." When I got up, they let go of their knees and stood up, too. They reminded me of how Musgrove had looked when the ambulance came for Balboa the day before: relieved.

I started to brush off my clothes. "Ooowww." I'd forgotten that I'd skidded on my palms, but the open cuts were there to remind me.

"Are you okay?" Tony asked yet again.

I'd be much better if you took me in your arms and

kissed me. That's what I *wanted* to say. But I'm not that stupid.

With my fingertips, I lifted my bike and walked it back toward the rack.

"That was the dumbest thing I've seen in a while," I heard Findlay say.

"It's not her fault. Maybe she was in a hurry, or maybe she needs glasses." Tony stuck up for me. My heart went ka-bong, ka-bong all the way into school.

I caught up with Merry at her locker and handed her the jar. "What's this?" she said.

"That's what I hope you can tell me." I explained where I'd found it and what it had to do with Balboa.

She pulled off the cap, sniffed it, then poured a drop onto her index finger. Next she rubbed her finger and thumb together to test the texture.

"Glycerin," she said.

"Just like that. You're sure?"

"Yup. They use it in lots of experiments, so most biology labs have some around. You know what else it's good for?"

She poured out another drop, then pressed her finger beneath each eye. When she pulled the finger away, there were two perfect teardrops. "Tears in the movies!" Next she smeared the teardrops to make it look like she'd been crying. "You didn't need me to tell you what it is. Anyone in the drama club could've told you."

The homeroom bell rang. Merry tried to wipe

the glycerin away, but she still looked wet under the eyes. "Don't get rid of it, Mer," I said. "Leave it there and maybe Mrs. Hatch will feel sorry for you and excuse you from class."

"I don't think so, Carter. See ya in biology."

I dropped off my piece about the Ambassadors, and left feeling good about meeting my deadline, and thinking, "That'll show Sheila what I can do when I get a decent assignment."

Traffic in the halls was moving slowly that morning. It wasn't just people putting off going to class. It was a clog around Adrian. Everyone was congratulating her, and probably also hoping she'd think about them when she picked the other two Ambassadors. I squeezed my way past the crowd surrounding her, feeling pleased with myself when I heard her shout hi to me through all those people.

I was surprised that Balboa showed up. But it seemed like she'd left part of her brain on the storage-room floor. She was moving slowly, and she sounded the way I do when I'm just waking after I've been up too late.

Linsey leaned forward and whispered, "Maybe she's on drugs."

"Hey, Mrs. Balboa," Judy Mancini called from the next desk over. "You better let those mice go." She meant the mice the juniors kept in a cage for animal behavior experiments. "I heard on the news this morning that the government is going to fine hospitals that use animals for experiments."

"Yeah," Corey Phipps added, blowing the hair out of her face, "we could report what goes on in here, and it could cost you a fortune."

Balboa looked bored. To be fair, she wasn't the only one. Judy and Corey were getting to be a major drag with their animal rights thing. I'm not against people having causes — I have a few, like outlawing cars so bikes can take over. But I don't spout off about them every five minutes.

"I heard that story, too," Balboa said. "And the hospital is being fined for gross neglect and cruelty, not for experimentation itself, which is still the most valuable and legitimate way of learning about various forms of life."

"I don't see what could be more gross or cruel than keeping animals in a box or slicing them open and taking them apart piece by piece."

"We've been through this before," Balboa said. "We have a philosophical difference. When you teach biology you can do whatever you want. But as long as you're in my class, you do things my way."

"If I were teaching biology, I'd use you as a specimen," Judy said under her breath, but not so far under that I couldn't hear it. "See how you like floating around in a jar of formaldehyde."

"Hey, Mrs. Balboa." Donny Gillespie had his hand up, but didn't wait to be called on. "Shouldn't you be home resting after your accident?"

"If I felt I should be at home, I'd be at home." She let her glasses slide down her nose. "Thank you for your concern." This was a big joke because everyone knew the only thing that concerned Donny was having a good time, something that was much easier with a substitute.

Balboa picked up her lesson-plan book and carried it with her to the blackboard. When she flipped the book open, pages went flying, landing at her feet and all along the front row.

"Oh my God!" Winnie Myers shrieked when she saw what those pages were. Pictures of men. Naked.

Everyone went scrambling to scoop them up. Everyone but Balboa, who took the yardstick off its hook and slammed it down on Owen Rinehart's desk. Owen jumped about a foot, and everyone else stopped dead. Under Balboa's stare, we crawled back to our desks.

"Page one-oh-four," she said, as if there weren't a full-color photo of a man with the dangling part of him hanging in full view, face up on the floor in front of her.

When the bell rang, everyone swooped for the pictures, including Merry, who came up with a blond guy with big shoulders, wearing nothing but a look that made me blush.

"I'm going to take him home for my mother," she said.

"Why, don't you want him? Looks like he wants you."

"Not my type."

"Of course. Not skinny enough."

"Poor Mrs. Balboa," she said once we'd left the classroom. "She must be so embarrassed."

"She didn't show it."

"But still, I bet she was. And on top of her accident yesterday."

"I wonder who put the pictures there."

"Probably Donny."

"Why?"

"Last week I heard him bragging about how he was going to steal porno magazines from his dad. And also, you know how he likes to bait Balboa."

"But why would his dad have porno magazines of men?"

Merry didn't have an answer. "Maybe it isn't him, then." She changed the subject. "You coming over to study tonight?" Merry and I had been studying for the big biology test together, which basically meant I asked lots of questions and Merry answered them.

"I don't think so. Art is supposed to call. I don't want to miss it. Tomorrow, though," I said.

There was a message for me when I got home, from Adrian. She'd picked Josh Dickerson as an Ambassador. Like Bob, Josh fit in with what Adrian had told me during the interview. He hadn't spent all of his time trying to become an Ambassador. He'd spent most of it working on electronics projects. I saw him mainly at assemblies, where he worked the lights or the projection equipment. He'd had his picture in the paper a few months before, when some gizmo he'd designed won first prize at a science fair.

All I knew besides that was that his mother was

Japanese and his father wasn't, which explained why his narrow, oval eyes were bright blue, and why he was twice as tall as the other Asian students at TAD.

Art didn't call, and Mom wouldn't let me try to reach him. "If he didn't call it's because he's too busy. He won't want you disturbing him," she said.

"But what if he just forgot?"

"If he forgot it's because he's too busy to remember. Just leave it alone, Carter. He'll call another night."

It wasn't the first time Art didn't do what he'd promised to do. You'd think I'd be used to it. But I still get disappointed.

I waited until Mom left the room and dialed his number.

"Can't come to the phone . . ." His machine. I hung up before his message was through. I tried to think what would make him too busy to remember to call me. Meetings. Whenever he wasn't writing one of his TV shows, he was in a meeting, talking about the show he had just written or the one he was going to write next. Art's show is about a detective in Los Angeles. That's one reason he moved to L.A. The other reason was the divorce; I heard Mom tell him she hoped he'd move far away so that she wouldn't have to.

The auditorium the next day was set up with rows of beige metal chairs for the Science Career Day assembly. The best thing about it was it was going to take three whole class periods.

"This'll be great," Merry said as we took our seats. We were assigned to the front row, which meant we'd have to pay attention.

"Don't count on it," I said. While I was glad to get out of class, I wasn't in the mood for listening to a bunch of nerds talk about microbes and galaxies. But then I remembered Merry wants to be a scientist.

"It probably will be great, for you."

"You're so close-minded it kills me," Merry said. She was right. Like Mom says, one of these days I'm going to have to realize I don't know it all.

Justin had told me about Balboa's Science Career Day. She plans it every year and invites guest speakers to talk about jobs where you have to be good in science. It was a way of trying to get us to work harder in her class; she thought we might try harder if we thought we'd get a good job at the end of it.

Whenever guests come to TAD, the head Ambassador is supposed to say a few words to greet them. So welcoming the Career Day speakers was Adrian's responsibility, her first as an Ambassador. She was waiting at the podium with a piece of paper, crunching it up, then smoothing it out. Josh was standing with her. I guess Adrian didn't realize the microphone was on because she said to him, "I'm so damn nervous."

Everyone heard, and after one long second, almost everyone cracked up. Except, of course, Balboa. She went to the podium, and knew enough to turn off the mike before she started in on Adrian.

Adrian didn't get to give the welcome after all. I tried to catch her eye so I could smile to cheer her up, but her head was down while she moved off to sit somewhere near the back.

Balboa switched the mike back on and began. After saying hello and thanking us for coming (as if we had any choice!) she introduced the first speaker. "You will probably accuse me of playing favorites, but the speaker I'm going to call to start us off is my husband, Dr. Richard Clarke."

Merry jabbed me with her elbow. "I wonder why his name is different from hers."

He looked tall standing next to her, but then, Balboa is on the short side. I shrugged. "Maybe she didn't change it, or maybe she was married before and didn't want to change it again."

Dr. Clarke put a transparency down on the projector beside the podium. "I have some charts here," he said, pointing at the projector, "showing the recent growth in government-sponsored careers in science—jobs that allow you to work in science and for the country at the same time." He switched on the projector, but nothing happened.

"You're not plugged in," Balboa said, looking for the cord, and then the socket. She found them, and about one second later she was sorry she had. The cord gave her a shock that made her jump about a foot back from the wall. She dropped the cord and rubbed her arm so the flesh shook like my aunt's Jell-O mold.

Dr. Clarke pulled her aside and patted her arm in a chummy way. He picked up the cord, took a look, then coiled it and put it on top of the projector.

"There seems to be an electrical problem. We'll have to do without the charts." He turned and smiled at Mrs. Balboa. "I was hoping my lecture would give you a charge." When she smiled back at him she looked like no one I'd ever seen before. Then I realized it's because I'd never seen her smile.

We had to sit through Dr. Clarke (who talked about looking for poisons in the water supply), a woman whose job is to go where people have died and say if they're really dead, and a guy who works in a rocket laboratory, before we took a break. I went straight for the transparency projector, but Tony Von Thelan beat me to it. I stood close to him, but *only* because there was no other way to see why it had given Balboa that shock.

Okay, so it wasn't the only reason. But it was a good excuse.

"Someone snipped through the plastic casing," he said, holding it out for me. I saw a neat square patch cut from the plastic covering the cord. Bright metal wires showed through.

"When she stuck this into the socket, her fingers were touching the metal on the cord. That's about the same as sticking your fingers in the socket," he said. "Pretty shocking!" He laughed at his own joke, and so did I, even though I didn't really think it was so funny. I read an article that said guys hate it if you don't laugh at their jokes.

"You're sure someone did this? It couldn't just happen?" I asked.

The look he gave me let me know he clearly thought he was dealing with an idiot. "No way," he said, and walked away. So much for laughing at his jokes.

After the assembly I found Justin and Adrian sitting together in the cafeteria. She still looked upset. "She was *trying* to embarrass me," Adrian was saying. They were so caught up in their conversation, neither even said hi to me.

"That's not true," Justin said gently, trying to defend Balboa and comfort Adrian at the same time. "She's not like that."

"You're the only one in school that feels that way about her. You'd think she'd respect me for trying to improve student-faculty relations. But instead, she has to humiliate me in front of everyone."

If I were Justin, I would've pointed out that Adrian did a pretty good job of humiliating herself by cursing into the microphone. But he only nodded.

"Well, Adrian," I said, "at least Balboa got paid back for kicking you off the platform." She looked at me, puzzled.

"What do you mean?" she said. Her voice was shaky.

"The electric shock. The accident was like punishment for Balboa," I said.

She smiled at that.

"Actually," I said, "I'm not so sure it *was* an

accident." I told them it looked like someone had messed with the projector cord.

"But nobody could have known that Balboa was going to be the one to plug it in," Justin said.

"That's right," Adrian said. "Everyone knows that Josh Dickerson sets up the equipment. If they were trying to get anyone, it would be Josh."

"Not if they got to it *after* Josh," I said, beginning to get ideas. "They could have unplugged it, messed with it, then left it for someone else — namely, Balboa — to plug in."

"I still don't get how they would know Balboa would be the one to do it," Adrian said.

"They took a chance," I said. "Maybe they've been to one of these things before and remembered that she stands up front."

Adrian's next question was for Justin. "What do you think?"

"I think Carter might be right."

This was a surprise. "Why?" I asked.

"I said she probably shouldn't take it seriously, but yesterday Mrs. Balboa told me someone's been calling her at night, making threats."

"Like what?" Adrian asked.

"Like she'd better watch it or she'd have an accident. She wouldn't tell me exactly what they said, but she wouldn't have said anything unless she was worried about it. And telling me may have been her way of asking me if I had any idea who might do something like that."

"Well," Adrian asked, "do you?"

"I know who it *could* be," I said. Adrian stopped twisting the ends of her hair and waited for me to go on. "It could be anyone who has Balboa. The way she grades, the way she hands out detentions like they were presents on Christmas, the way she puts everyone down . . . it *could* be almost anyone."

CHAPTER 5

I was heading for the bike rack when I noticed Mrs. Balboa standing by her old Dodge Dart. She was digging through her purse, pulling all the junk out of it and piling it onto the hood.

Bob Earle saw her, too, and while I stood and stared, he went up to her. "Something wrong, Mrs. Balboa?"

"I seem to have lost my keys."

"Did you leave them back in the classroom?"

"I doubt it. But I might have."

"I'll go back with you and help you look for them," I said. She looked at me like "*You*, Carter Colborn, Delinquent — *you* are offering to help me?" I have to admit — I wasn't just trying to be helpful. I wanted a chance to talk to her about some of the things that had been happening to her lately, for my newspaper article.

With her bad leg Balboa had a hard time climbing the steps to her room. Ordinarily she'd take the special elevator TAD has for disabled students and teachers. But you need a key to get into it, and keys were what Balboa didn't have.

On the slow walk to the room, I mentioned the frog in her lunch, the threatening phone calls, the fall in the closet, the pictures in her lesson book, and the electric shock. But when we reached the room she just shrugged. "Some — obviously — were pranks. Others were accidents. I've never met a teacher who wasn't the victim of pranks at one time or another. And I don't know a single person who has managed to live to be my age without having a few accidents." She paused a second, then added, "You're not looking for my keys."

I looked over her desk, through her trash can, and in the storage closet. "Do you have any idea where you left them?"

"I was sure I'd dropped them into my purse," she said. I was going to suggest she was still confused from her concussion, but I decided against it.

Bob Earle stuck his head in the door. "I got your car started up for you," he said. "Hot-wired it," he explained. "Just in case your keys don't turn up."

That was a real Ambassador thing to do, all right. She thanked him. "You'll have to show me how to turn it off so I'll know what to do when I get home," she said. "Good thing I have another set there. I have to come back here to do some work this evening."

I followed them outside, to my bike. I was supposed to have met Merry at the library half an hour before, and I knew she'd be going nuts wondering where I was.

I told her about Balboa's missing keys. "Carter, *everyone* loses their keys at least once in a while."

"But don't you think there are a lot of coincidences here?" I went through the list of everything that'd happened to Balboa, starting with the frog.

"I still think you're making a big deal out of nothing," she said, picking up her pencil and filling something in on a graph she was making.

As usual I wasn't quite ready to get to work. "Remember you said you wondered why Balboa's name is different from her husband's?"

"Yes . . ."

"I know how we can find out."

"I think you would be better off trying to find out about photosynthesis."

"It'll only take a second," I lied.

Merry pushed her graph aside and followed me to the reference librarian's desk.

I asked for the indexes for our town newspaper, the *St. Davids Tribune*. You look up someone's name in the index and it'll tell you when the paper ran a story about him. The indexes go back seventy years, so you can find out who was getting married, getting elected, getting killed, or just getting in trouble, all the way back to 1917.

We went through the indexes for the 1980s, and didn't find anything under "Balboa." Then we started on the 1970s. "Balboa weds Clarke!" Merry sounded as if she'd won the lottery. The date in the index was 5/28/79.

I told the librarian we wanted to see that paper. She gave it to me on a reel of microfilm, which I threaded onto a projection machine that looked like a computer screen. I switched on the light, and we were in business.

I moved the pages along until I reached May 28.

" 'Beverly Balboa Weds,' " Merry read. " 'The small ceremony was held at St. Augustine's, with a reception afterward at the home of the bride and groom. The bride is a science teacher with the local school system. The groom, Dr. Richard Clarke, is a toxicologist with the United States Environmental Protection Agency. It is a second marriage for both. The bride, who was widowed five years ago, will keep her previous married name. The groom's first marriage ended in divorce.' "

We went to the index for 1974 to see if there was a story that would tell us what had happened to make Balboa a widow.

There was.

" 'Car crash kills two leaves third injured,' " I read. "God, Mer, this is the worst," I said before I went on with the piece. " 'At approximately nine thirty last night, a car driven by Mr. Arnold Balboa swerved to avoid a bicyclist, and crashed into a telephone pole outside his home.

" 'Tragically, Mr. Balboa and his twelve-year-old son, Joel, died in the crash. His wife, Beverly

Balboa, also a passenger, is listed in serious condition at St. Davids Medical Center. Doctors there say she is being treated for shock and will require surgery on her left leg as a result of the crash. The cyclist, fifteen-year-old Carole Markin, was unharmed.' "

Merry stared, stunned. And I sat there kicking myself for all the mean things I'd ever thought or said about Balboa.

"So much for the story about the snakebite, huh?" I said. "Now we know what really happened to her leg."

"Yeah" was all Merry could manage for a moment. "You know, part of me wishes we had never found out," she said while I shut off the machine. "But it'll help us understand her better."

I agreed. "Maybe the reason she's so hard on us is because she wants us to take life more seriously, since her son didn't get to live his."

"Maybe," Merry said.

We tried to study, but it was a lost cause.

"Whose Honda is that out front?" Usually the strange cars at our house meant some new guy was visiting my mother. But Mom was in the kitchen alone.

"It's Adrian's. She says her parents bought it for her, as a present for winning the debate championship."

"What will you buy *me* when I become some kind of champion?"

"Depends on what kind of champion. Right

now you'd qualify for wise guy, in which case you don't deserve anything except a sudsy mouth-wash."

"So, what's Adrian doing here, anyway?"

"She's helping your brother write letters for summer jobs. It's some deal they've got going — he helps her with biology, she helps him with the letters. Justin's very excited about it; he says she's a persuasive person. I guess that's why she's a debate champion."

And in they came. Justin went for the refrigerator, while Adrian hopped onto a high swivel chair at the counter.

"How's it going?" Mom asked.

"It *would* be going fine," Adrian said, "only he's being way too modest. I keep telling him the only point in writing these letters is to brag about your-self."

"She's right, Justin," Mom said.

"I know." He reached for the milk. "I just hate to sound like a show-off."

"It so happens you have plenty to show off about," Mom said.

"Yeah, like being related to me," I said.

Adrian laughed, but Mom and Justin just rolled their eyes.

"Someone stole Balboa's keys," I said.

"How do you know?" Justin took a swig from the carton.

"They disappeared from where she'd put them."

"How do you know she didn't just lose them?" Adrian asked.

"A hunch. With everything that's been happening to her . . ."

"Last week you couldn't stand that teacher," Mom said, "now you're obsessed with her. I can't keep up with you."

"Listen to this," I said, then told them about the *Tribune* story.

"That's *horrible*," Adrian said. "Now I feel awful about the things I said after the assembly. Someone should stop whoever's been playing those pranks on her. She's suffered enough."

"Sounds like something the Ambassadors could do," Justin said.

"We will as soon as your sleuthing sister finds out who we should go after." Adrian checked her watch. "I've got to go grab dinner before practice. The school board was using the auditorium after school, so we had to schedule rehearsal for tonight."

"Call me when it's over. I'll be working on the letters, and I'll want to read some stuff back to you," Justin said, walking her toward the door.

"Okay," she said. "That'll be around ten."

I had to hold myself back from spying on the kind of good-bye they gave each other.

After dinner I tried to write my Balboa story. But I couldn't concentrate. When I first thought up the piece, it was supposed to be about an *accident*. But now it seemed like something else.

What kind of student would harass Balboa? A student that wanted to get back at her, maybe. But for what? Grades would be the most obvious thing.

What clues did I have? Donny and his porno magazines; Judy and Corey and their animal rights. And there could be someone else, someone I wasn't even thinking of. Someone who was getting bad grades from Balboa and wanted to give her something in return.

There was a way of finding out who that might be. Even if it wasn't strictly legal, it was a way.

I called Neil. He wouldn't like my plan. But even so, he'd help me with it.

CHAPTER 6

Neil was stunned by my idea, which was to sneak into the school office and go through the files to find out which students were getting bad grades from Balboa. Anyone who was failing badly enough could be a suspect.

"Are you serious?" he said. "I haven't checked into it lately, but the last I knew, it was against the law."

I knew that, I told him. But if we were really careful, we wouldn't get caught. "Besides, it's for a good cause."

"I don't know . . ."

"I'm going to do it whether you come or not." I knew that would get him; Neil would do anything to prove he's not a wimp.

"All right," he said. "But if we get caught, my bail's on you." We agreed to meet in ten minutes.

*   *   *

"Any bets on who it is?" Neil asked once we were on our way. He'd followed my instructions and worn dark clothes.

"I've got a few ideas, but I'm not going to bet on any of them," I said.

"I think it's Von Findlay," he said.

That was not one of my ideas. "What on earth makes you say that?"

"Who was bounced off the lacrosse team last semester because he flunked Balboa's class?"

"Peter Findlay. . . . But I don't see how you can . . ."

"Who rushed up to look at the electrical cord on the projector?"

"Tony Von Thelan . . ."

"Does a criminal wait around for people to decide he's not guilty? No. He goes right to the scene of the crime so no one will suspect him. That's what Von Thelan did. He went to look at that cord so he could say, 'Gee, look what *someone* did,' and no one would ever think *he* was the one."

"But why would he be after Balboa?" I asked.

"Because when Findlay catches cold, Von Thelan sneezes."

"Translation, please."

"Von Thelan reacts to anything that happens to Findlay. Since Balboa got Findlay booted from the team, Von Thelan would help him get back at her . . . especially if Findlay's grades could keep him off the team next year, too."

Maybe Neil had a point. But I couldn't take his suspicions too seriously. First, there was the way

I felt about Tony. Second, Neil knew the way I felt about Tony. In other words, I was sure Neil wanted me to think Tony was guilty so I would drop him.

At about ten thirty we reached the school.

"Now what?" Neil's face looked even pastier under the streetlight.

"Now we sneak in."

"How?"

"The drama club was practicing here tonight; they had to get in somehow." I took a chance on the door closest to the auditorium. It worked.

And there we were, with the whole school to ourselves. It wasn't anything like it was during the day. It made me realize that what makes a school *your* school is the people who go there. Even if you hate them. After I graduate, when I don't know anyone who goes there anymore, TAD will probably feel the way it did that night.

"What am I doing here?" Neil asked. "I can't think of a single book where the detective doesn't get nabbed, if not *stabbed,* trying to get away with something like this." But he knew what he was doing there . . . he came along to be alone with me in the dark. He reached for my hand.

I pretended not to see it coming and moved ahead of him through the cafeteria into Musgrove's office.

There had been a few lights on in the cafeteria, but it was pitch-black in the office.

Neil's fingers went for the light switch. *"Don't!"* I warned him.

"Sorry," he said. "Wasn't thinking. I haven't been this nervous since my Bar Mitzvah."

I pulled my flashlight from my bag and started to shine it around. "Sshh!" Neil said, clamping his hand over the flashlight to block the beam. "Did you hear that?" I froze to listen.

"Hear what?" I said after a few seconds.

"I know I heard somebody laughing."

I yanked my flashlight clear of his hand. "You're just trying to scare me out of this," I said. "And it won't work."

"I swear I heard something, Carter."

"And I swear I didn't." Neil shrugged, and I beamed the light around until it found the office computer.

"Do you know how to work this model?" Clearly, Neil didn't.

"I think so. It looks just like the one Art has." I hit a switch on the side. It blipped and beeped, and the screen went bright green.

"Pretty good," Neil said. "Now what?"

"Now, I start guessing." I hit the same three keys I would have used if I were on Art's computer. "All right!" I got what I wanted — a list of the information inside the computer.

"Yeah, but what does it mean?" Neil said, leaning over me to look.

Good question. It was in code. ALXMRHS, KLYGD, DNLSHA . . .

"Shucks, and we forgot the decoder ring, Sherlock," Neil said cheerfully. He thought we'd have to give up and go.

"But we can figure it out," I said. He wasn't cheerful anymore.

"Let's try S-G-R-D — that might be code for 'student grades.' "

No luck. It turned out to be "salary gradation."

"How about S-R-C-R-D-S. Maybe it's 'student records.' "

Nope. I was right about the "records" part, but it was *service* records — a list of electricians and repairmen who work for the school.

"If we have to go through that whole list, we'll be here until homeroom tomorrow." Neil really wanted to get out. And I was starting to feel guilty about dragging him into it.

"Okay. Just one more try . . . S-F-L-S. Could be 'student files.' "

It was.

"Let's look at Findlay and Von Thelan first," Neil said.

"Why?"

"To check my theory. I want to show you how right I am."

I figured I owed him something for going along with me, so, after praying under my breath that he was wrong, I scrolled to Findlay's grades.

"C minus, D, D, F, D," Neil read from the screen. "That's how you spell 'trouble,' all right."

But Findlay's trouble was nothing compared with the trouble that was coming our way.

My eyes weren't prepared for the overhead lights, but Musgrove didn't care about my sensitive vision. He charged at us, gripping us each by the arm and rattling us so our teeth clicked like castanets. He let go and looked at the screen, and shut off the computer, sputtering like a lunatic the whole time.

Neil looked petrified. Not that I was exactly calm. How would I explain this? My good intentions weren't enough. I wondered why I hadn't seen that before.

Musgrove got on the phone. He still hadn't said a word to us. He was so upset I wondered if he would make sense when he finally spoke. Unfortunately, he did.

"Captain, this is Walter Musgrove at Thomas A. Dooley High School. I have apprehended two trespassers in the principal's office. Would you send a car for them?"

Neil took my hand. His felt as slimy and cold as a wet lizard. Even so, I squeezed it to give him courage. Not that I had much to share at the moment.

Once the cop arrived, I distracted myself from what was happening by looking him over. He didn't look much older than Justin. He was even pretty cute. Maybe I could make friends with him, get him to stop for a burger, then convince him to drop us off at home instead of taking us to the station.

No luck. First of all, Musgrove was tailing us in his car. Second, the cop wasn't exactly Mr. Conversation. "So, you get many calls like this?" I asked once we were settled in the black and white — me and Neil in the back, behind the wire mesh that's supposed to keep dangerous felons from bonking the driver on the head.

"Some," he said.

"Oh really?" I said, trying to imagine how Adrian would conduct this kind of conversation. Then I realized that Adrian would never *have* to conduct this kind of conversation. "Give me an example."

"Can't think of one right now."

I leaned over to Neil and whispered, "A real regular guy, huh?"

Neil tried to smile, but it came off like he was sick to his stomach.

I could see the cop watching me in the rearview mirror. Maybe he thought Neil and I were plotting to hijack his squad car. Little did he know we had already used all our guts back at school and had none left for anything like that.

The police station is one of the oldest buildings in town, which is depressing when you think about it: the first thing they did when they started this town was to figure out what to do with the crooks.

Anyway, the place is old, with high ceilings and beige waxed floors. It smells of old building and cigarette smoke, and there are wooden benches along the corridor where everyone who ever waited there has carved his name. Some had to wait so long they had time to add their girlfriend's or boyfriend's name plus a comment about them. When we sat down, I rested my elbow on "Carol + Mike."

I was thinking about what I would scratch into the wood when Musgrove arrived. The police officer took us to the captain, who stared at us from behind a desk where he was chewing on a ballpoint pen.

"I won't be pressing charges, Captain," Musgrove said.

I think I breathed for the first time since we'd been caught.

"We can handle this at school. I hope you didn't mind bringing them in here just to shake them up a bit."

"Not at all." The captain pulled the pen from his mouth and stared at me. "You look awfully sweet to be prowling around the principal's office this time of night."

"She may *look* sweet, but she's got a discipline record stretching from here to Philadelphia," Musgrove told him. "We're going to release report cards soon, and I would guess she was in there trying to raise her grades. And if I hadn't been there to lock up after the drama club, she might have gotten away with it."

So *that's* what he thought. Neil looked startled, and was about to correct him. I jabbed him with my elbow and shook my head, warning him to keep his mouth shut. I knew enough about the law to know that it was a lot worse to be caught looking at other people's records than messing with your own.

And as if to prove he really *was* going to punish us in some way, Musgrove turned to me and said,

"I'm going to put together a special committee for a hearing to decide if you should be allowed back at school next year."

Oh great. Boarding school, here I come.

The captain told us to call our parents. I would have preferred to talk to Art, but I was in enough trouble without giving the cops a long-distance phone bill. I dialed Mom.

Justin answered. "Hey!" I said, as if I were calling from Disney World. "Guess where I am?"

"Wherever it is, you'd better come home," he said. "Mom is going into her tenth fit."

"I can't come home, Justin. Unless Mom comes to get me."

"She's not in the mood to get you, unless maybe with a shotgun."

"Well," I said, "tell her there are plenty of people with pistols around here."

"Carter, where are you?"

I told him.

"Maybe I'd better come for you. We'll make up something to tell Mom."

"That's the trouble, Just," I said. "They say it's got to be Mom. They won't let me go with you."

Neil's mother showed up first. She didn't say anything, but I could tell by the look she gave me, I wasn't her favorite person in the world.

When we reached the car, Mom started in on me. "I bet I know what you were up to in there. Playing Nancy Drew. Am I right?"

"Well, yes." I tried to wedge some more words

in before she started up again. "It's an important case —"

"Nancy Drew had a lawyer for a father to get her out of trouble, which is a lot more than you've got going for you. And by the way, your father called while you were out."

All the way home, she hammered away: I was a humiliation to her; she was having a hard enough time getting along in St. Davids; how could I do this to her when I knew everything she'd gone through with the divorce; I was grounded for every weekend until my hearing; I was to drop the case immediately; and — like I knew she'd say — boarding school was her only alternative.

I don't always know when to keep my mouth shut, but I knew then.

"Your only real hope, it seems to me, is to solve this case," Art said. I didn't tell him that Mom had told me to drop it. "You have to impress those clodheads so much they'll forgive you this trespass — excuse the pun."

"You think that would work?"

"If you can prove that your intentions were good, *and* that you stuck with the case and got results . . . I'd be surprised if it didn't." He paused. "Now, here's the lecture."

"I knew it was coming," I groaned.

"One of the first rules my detectives follow," he said, meaning his TV detectives, "is to stay within the law. As soon as they break the law, they're no better than the crooks they're trying to catch.

"You have to be a lot smarter and work a lot harder to do your job within the law. It's like — it's easier to win a game if you cheat, but you need skill and smarts to win playing by the rules. You get what I'm saying, hon?"

"Yes, Art."

"And you'll keep that in mind while you find out who's pestering Balboa?"

"Yes."

"Call me if you need me."

"I miss you, Daddy."

"I miss you too, Carterkid. And Carter," he added, "go easy on your mother. She cares about you just as much as I do, and she deserves a lot of respect for putting up with you day in and day out." He was only half joking at the end there.

"I know. I'll try."

CHAPTER 7

I called Neil to apologize and to see how things were going at his house. The phone rang for a long time; I was about to hang up when a groggy voice said, "Hello?"

The voice reminded me of something I had completely forgotten: the time. It was after midnight.

"I'm sorry to wake you, Mrs. Weinstein. This is Carter. I guess I'll just talk to Neil tomorrow."

When she spoke again, she sounded more awake. "Neil's father and I don't want him to have anything to do with you, outside of school. That's all I have to say. Good-bye."

I didn't have a chance to get a word in before she hung up. But that was okay — there was nothing to say but "I'm sorry," and that wouldn't have changed anything.

Even though it was late, I couldn't fall asleep. So I tried to work on my piece. Maybe thinking about Balboa's troubles would help get my mind off my own. But I didn't have enough evidence to write the article. No matter what Neil thought, Findlay's grades weren't proof of anything. Lots of people get bad grades, and they don't have their best friends go after their teacher. It'd take a lot more than Findlay's bad grades to convince me that Tony Von Thelan had anything to do with it.

Since I couldn't write, I tried reading. But I couldn't concentrate. So I just lay there imagining what it would be like to be Adrian and have everyone like me. That didn't work, either.

I was up all night.

Riding to school the next day seemed to take forever. Time always drags when you have something awful to think about, like what a horrible day it would be. First, everyone would know about my probably getting expelled. That's the kind of thing that gets around without your even knowing how.

Second, there was going to be the big test review. If Balboa called on me, what was I going to tell her — "I didn't study because I was reading your old wedding announcements"?

The day started out just as I'd expected. "Heard about what happened to you and Neil last night," Linsey said by my locker.

"Good for you," I said. It occurred to me that if it hadn't been for her and that detention I might never have gotten into this mess.

"Don't be so defensive," she said.

I could've said something, but I let it go.

Then Merry showed. "Did you see who's in Musgrove's office?" Obviously she hadn't heard about my trouble. I shook my head. "There's a policeman, *and* Dr. Clarke. Balboa's husband. And he looks awful, like he's been there all night."

"Well, he hasn't," I said. I explained how I would have known if he *had* been there all night.

"That was a stupid thing to do," Merry said. "And poor Neil. That silly boy would do *anything* for you."

"Don't rub it in."

She didn't. "What do you think Dr. Clarke is doing here . . . with a policeman?"

"I don't know . . . unless something's happened to Balboa."

Which, when biology class came, looked like a real possibility: we had a substitute.

She was tall and big, with blond hair piled on top of her head like a small trash barrel, and she was setting up a film projector. No one was bothering with their assigned seats. I grabbed one beside Tony. Judy and Corey sat down behind us.

"Did you see what they're going to serve at lunch today?" Judy said to Corey as she lit a Camel behind her book. "Liquefied cow cadaver."

Sloppy joes.

"Gag," Corey said.

When the bell rang, Donny shook a can of Coke and let it spray out like champagne.

"I doubt your teacher lets you do that in class," the substitute said.

"Oh yes she does," Tony said. "It's an experiment in thermodynamics."

Donny probably didn't know what thermodynamics was, but he nodded anyway.

The film was about the bloodstream, which we weren't even studying. Everyone screamed whenever they showed blood, which was practically all the time.

In other words, it was a typical day with a substitute.

Topping it off, Judy and Corey decided to "liberate" the mice. Liberation involved opening their cages and letting them go.

"Now there's plenty of room in the cage for Balboa if she ever makes it back," Judy said.

"I hope she doesn't," Corey added.

The way Winnie Myers screamed, you'd think the mice were man-eating monsters. The substitute slammed the door to keep them from escaping, and half the class stood up on their chairs while the other half got onto the floor to scamper after the mice. Meanwhile, Judy and Corey chanted, "Let them go! Let them go!" Then the bell rang and everybody flew out, probably including the mice.

The hall was packed, and I had to wedge my way through the crowd to discover why. Everyone was watching Balboa being helped out of the elevator by Musgrove on one side and her husband on the other.

"I heard she's been there all night." Neil squeezed in next to me and whispered like he was afraid his mother might catch him talking to me.

Balboa looked rickety standing there, like she might just collapse . . . splat. But she leaned hard on her husband.

"Everyone." It was Adrian, at her pep squad best. "Please clear the hall so Mrs. Balboa can get through and get some air." People grumbled, but they left. Not me, of course. I was going to get the full story.

No one could tell it better than the school custodian, Mr. Herlihy. Mr. Herlihy likes helping me. I think it's because I kidded him once and said my father could get him on television — and he took me seriously. The truth is he *would* make a real character just playing himself. He's built like a ladder, tall and narrow, and he's got thick white hair that hangs into his eyes, which are blue — although it's hard to see them with the lids drooping over them like hoods.

"Looks to me," he said, "like somebody got the key to the control box and locked her in."

"But she had to have a key to get in, right?" I asked. "So why couldn't she use it to get out?"

"Because," he said, "the control box is out here, and she was in there. The key works from the outside."

That's why someone had stolen her keys. To trap her in the elevator.

I asked Mr. Herlihy if I could look into the elevator.

"If you want," he said.

He twisted the key and the doors slid open.

I didn't have to search long. The one and only clue stared straight at me the moment I stepped inside.

It was a snake, painted on the wall, with its tongue lashing out like it meant it. And there was something else.

Across the tongue, in blood-dripping letters, were the words AMBASSADORS OF DOOM. And underneath that, much smaller, someone had written "Balboa Beware, AOD," in red felt-tip pen.

Mr. Herlihy wheeled a bucket out of the storage closet next to the elevator. I asked him not to wash down the wall until my friends had seen it. I told him I'd bring Neil and Merry around during lunch.

"Gotcha," he said, winking.

Neil borrowed a camera from one of the *TAD Times* photographers. But by the time the three of us got to the elevator, the door was shut and stuck with a sign: OFF LIMITS.

"I can't believe this," I said, and started studying the setup to see how we could get around it.

Neil saw what I was up to, and stuck his arm out to block me. "No you don't, Carter," he said. "Not after last night."

He was right. After all, one reason for examining the clue in the elevator was to get *out* of the trouble we'd gotten into the night before. The other reason, of course, was to help Balboa.

"Go right ahead," Mr. Herlihy called from behind us. "This doesn't mean you," he said, pulling the sign away and waving it around. "It's for all the others." He stuck his key into the control box and, again, the doors opened.

Neil raised the camera to take a shot. "Be sure to get the handwriting good and clear," I said. "It can be a dead giveaway."

Next, Merry scraped at the paint, letting the chips fall into a vial. She'd find a way to tell what kind of paint it was; then it'd be up to me to figure out who might have used it.

"Carter, could we see you a minute?" Adrian was standing with Josh Dickerson just outside the elevator. I went over to them. "Someone's making fun of us, right? Why else would they call themselves *Ambassadors* and do something like *that*?" She pointed at the elevator. Josh nodded. I looked at him and wondered why I'd never noticed how cute he was.

That someone was making fun of the Ambassadors seemed obvious. "I think you're right," I said. "Someone's got a sick sense of humor."

"Sick, all right," Josh said. He seemed shy. When I looked at him, he looked down.

"Everyone's talking about what's been happening to Balboa and why can't the Ambassadors do anything about it . . ."

"Yeah, we look really stupid," Josh said, although it looked like an effort for him.

"It's not the best way to start off," Adrian added. Josh was about to strain himself again to say something else, but he was saved by the p.a. system. "Attention." It was Musgrove. "Carter Colborn to the office. Carter Colborn to the office, please."

"What's that about?" Adrian asked.

Although I assumed it had something to do with my expulsion hearing, I shrugged and said, "I don't know."

There was a new bulletin board display outside Musgrove's office: TAD AMBASSADORS, with Adrian's picture at the top, and Josh, and Bob underneath. I stopped to look at them, more to stall than anything else. Once I figured I'd kept him waiting long enough, I went in.

Someone else was already there. Donny Gillespie. Donny is a runt — even Neil is bigger than him. In fact, Neil once said Donny's picture could run in the dictionary next to the word *puny*. Like a lot of small guys, Donny was always trying to prove himself. And like most guys who try to prove themselves, he was always getting into trouble for it.

"I told you, you can go," Musgrove said.

"Okay, okay." Donny got up slowly, like a rundown windup toy. He looked at me and rolled his eyes, as a comment on Musgrove.

Musgrove ran his hand over his face and shook his head. "I could do more than expel you for this," he said. "I could have you locked up in Youth Authority. Put away! Don't look at me like you don't know what I'm talking about."

"But I don't."

"You don't." He ran his hand over his face

again and leaned back. "You don't know anything about the elevator? How Mrs. Balboa just happened to be locked in on the very night I caught you trespassing on these premises?"

"What?" He couldn't be serious.

"Please. Don't play dumb with me." He *was* serious. "Mrs. Balboa said she found herself stuck in there at ten fifteen last night. And who happened to be caught trespassing at ten forty-five? I'll give you a clue. She's the same one who can't get decent grades without breaking into her records to change them."

"But," I said, my voice cracking worse than Neil's, which was changing, "talk to Mrs. Balboa. She'll tell you I've been trying to help her. Just yesterday I helped her look for her keys."

Musgrove smiled, but not because he was happy to hear I was innocent. "A guilty person often seems helpful. It's a way of disguising her guilt." That's what Neil had said about Von Thelan.

"How can I prove I didn't do it?"

"Your hearing is coming up. You can try to defend yourself then."

CHAPTER 8

I went straight to the bathroom. Before even checking to see if I was making a jerk of myself in front of anybody, I cried. I cried the way I cried when Art left for Los Angeles. In other words, I really cried.

I moved into a stall to blow my nose, and to hide. If someone came in, she'd want to know what was wrong, and I'd have to make something up, like I'd just learned I'd been kidnapped as a baby and now I had to move in with my real parents who were math teachers in Iowa.

I heard the grunt of the bathroom door opening. Voices followed.

"Is your mom going to drive us?"

"No. She says she won't drive me anywhere this week."

"Why not?"

"Because she heard me tell Danny I'd throw a match in his hair. Lit."

I peeked through the crack between the door and the stall. It was Judy and Corey. They were combing their hair and putting black rims over and under their eyes.

"You're sick."

"I was only kidding. And, anyway, look who's talking!"

"What've *I* done?" Judy asked, drawing it out so you could tell she'd definitely done *something*.

They both cracked up. And I thought maybe I knew what that something was . . . something like locking a teacher in an elevator. After all, hadn't they said they wanted Balboa to know what it was like to be stuck in a cage?

"So I guess we're *walking* to the mall, huh?"

"I guess."

The door grunted again, and they were gone.

After school I caught Merry outside her locker and tried to convince her to go to the mall with me. "Isn't there something you want to buy?"

"There are lots of things I'm trying *not* to buy," she said. "If I spend any more money . . ."

"Don't bring any money, then."

"Then why should I go?"

"To help me out."

"Like Neil helped you out? No thanks, Carter."

"This is all perfectly legal, I promise," I said.

Then I explained that I wanted to follow Judy and Corey, but I needed her to switch off with me so I wouldn't be conspicuous.

"All right," she said. "But please don't try anything cute."

We half walked, half ran in the direction of the mall, until we could see Judy and Corey ahead of us. They were hard to miss. Every day they dressed in black — different outfits, but always black. It looked all right on Judy, whose hair was the color of new pennies. But it made Corey, with her pasty skin, look like a skunk.

We slowed down to tail them. When they went into Bloomingdale's, I got set to follow.

"As soon as they come out," I said to Merry, "you pick up the trail. I'll follow from a distance and take up after their next stop. Here." I handed her a Walkman.

"What's this for?"

"It's for going like this," I said, sticking the headphones on and bobbing my head. "Just don't turn it on. They'll think you can't hear them."

Merry rolled her eyes.

I went into Bloomingdale's, where Judy and Corey were having a shoot-out with spray cologne. A woman behind the counter in a white smock wasn't frantic yet, but she was close. "Young ladies, I must ask you to stop." The woman had black hair that looked like it had been waxed, and a face that looked pretty much the same way. She was ready to duck behind her counter if they turned the weapons on her — no way she wanted to smell like what she was selling.

"I'm going to call security," she said. I wanted to see that. A burly security officer drenched in Jonquil Mist.

But I never got the chance. They stopped, put down the bottles, and headed out.

"She's trying to look young," Judy said so the black-haired lady could hear. "But she's got to be at least thirty."

"My grandmother looked better than that the last time I saw her," Corey said. "And that was at her *wake*."

The black-haired woman pressed her lips together, and shook her head.

Merry was waiting, bobbing in the Walkman just as I'd told her. "They're all yours," I said.

"*What?*"

Not just as I'd told her. She had the Walkman *on*. I pushed the "stop" button.

"I said follow them now, please."

She started after them. Then she stopped.

"What now?" I said.

"What am I supposed to be watching for?"

"You're supposed to listen . . . to hear if they say anything about Balboa."

She was off again. I watched her follow them into Dress for Less. About ten minutes later, she followed them out.

"Nothing," she said when I asked her what she'd heard. "But it's partly my fault."

"Oh yeah?" I said.

"I grabbed something off the rack so I could follow them into the dressing room." She stopped.

"Go on," I said.

"I got into the dressing room next to them, but when they tried on their clothes, they left to look in the big mirror at the end of the hall."

"Didn't you follow them?"

She shook her head.

"Why not?"

"The thing I'd grabbed off the rack turned out to be a maternity dress. I would've looked stupid trying it on."

It was my turn to roll my eyes.

"By the way, Carter" — Merry wanted to get off the subject — "they went that-a-way."

The way she meant was into an art-supply store; when I got there, they were looking at paints.

"This is the color I'll use when I paint your portrait," Judy said. I squinted to see what she meant. It was mustard yellow.

"You're sick," Corey said.

"I'm accurate," Judy replied.

"And this is the color I'd use for you." Corey held out pea green.

"But you can't paint, jerko."

"True."

"Let's see," Judy said. "I need this, this, this, and definitely this. And this would be nice." She was pointing to various colors. She leaned to whisper something to Corey. I didn't catch a word.

Then Corey went to the counter to ask for help

picking an easel from the selection at the back of the store. Meanwhile, Judy went to work. Two by two, she dropped tubes of paint into her shoulder bag.

A second later, she was out of there.

The right thing to do would have been to report her. The right thing would have been to walk up to the salesman and tell him he'd been ripped off.

But I didn't do it. I wasn't thinking. Or I *was* thinking, but only about how much I wanted to nail them for what they'd done to Balboa — not for stealing some paints.

I checked the brand of paint she'd taken. I'd come back later to buy a tube so Merry could compare it with the samples from the elevator.

When I got back out, Merry was talking to a tall, thin guy. Bob Earle. "Oh, hi, Carter," she said, in a voice that was at least twice as high as the one she normally used. "You know Bob, don't you?"

"Yes," I said. "Hi." This was no time for Merry to be flirting.

"I was just congratulating Bob on becoming an Ambassador."

"Merry," I said, "where are our *friends?*"

She covered her mouth with both hands.

"I've got to go," Bob said. "Good to see you guys."

"We lost them," I said.

"*I* lost them." Merry was apologetic.

"I hope it was worth it. Did he ask you out?"

Merry shook her head.

We decided to get something to eat. Luckily

for us, Judy and Corey had decided the same thing. We got in line behind them at Big Burger.

"How would you like it if someone ground you up and sizzled you on hot grease?" Judy said to the pimply guy who'd asked her what she'd like. He wasn't sharp enough to come back at her. "How can you get up in the morning knowing you're going to spend the day chucking slabs of cow onto a fryer?"

We watched them go from place to place. We didn't have to follow them to know that they were saying pretty much the same thing wherever they went.

Meanwhile, Merry and I got muffins at Petite Bakerie, and waited for the Dreadful Duo to move on.

I followed them into Pets!Pets!Pets! The first thing they did was ask the guy there how he'd like to be kept in a cage the size of a shoe box. He ignored them.

Then they went down the row of caged dogs and cats, just looking. They watched the saleslady hand a puppy over to a six-year-old kid, and, like she did in the art-supply store, Judy leaned to whisper something to Corey. At first I thought of the mice in biology class, and imagined them "liberating" the animals in the store.

But what they had in mind was even worse.

They waited for the kid's mother to go to the counter to pay for the dog. Then they pounced.

"I wouldn't take that dog home if I were you," Judy said to the kid.

"I wouldn't either," Corey added. " 'Cause you

know what's going to happen when it gets bigger?"

The kid shook his head.

"It's going to get so hungry that dog food won't be enough for it."

The kid didn't get it. So Judy made it clear.

"It's going to eat *you*."

"Your mother is buying that dog because she wants to get rid of you," Corey said.

The kid dropped the dog and froze. Judy and Corey took off. I couldn't tell for sure, but I'd be willing to bet they were laughing their heads off.

The puppy was scampering toward the door, and I grabbed him before he could make it into the mall. I tried to hand him back to the kid, who was using his mother's skirt the way I used to use our living-room drapes when we played hide-and-seek.

"Those girls were lying," I said. "This is a nice dog. It would never eat you."

The boy's mother looked at me like I was dangerously nuts. But I didn't bother to explain. I hugged the puppy and petted it until the kid got the idea. I turned the dog over to him and split.

Merry was waiting. I told her it was time to quit. I was sick of Judy and Corey. And even though we didn't have definite proof they had done anything to Balboa, at least we knew they were mean enough to have tried.

We went by the art-supply store and chipped in for a tube of paint. Then we went home.

Since I was grounded for the weekend, I tried to forget it was Friday night. The easiest way to forget was to do homework, which I'd normally put off until Sunday. The biology test would be Monday. Now was my chance to be responsible for a change and not wait until the last possible minute to study.

While I was looking over my notes, an advantage of going to boarding school occurred to me. I'd get away from Mom's parties. This one was so loud I could barely hear the phone ring, or Merry's voice on the end of the line.

"I've compared the samples, and the paint from the mall isn't the kind that was used in the elevator," she said. "I checked the paints they use at school, and it isn't from there either. The only other thing I can tell you is that it's a really rich paint. I called the art store and the guy said the richer the paint the more expensive it is — up to twenty dollars a tube." We'd paid only five.

Someone knocked on my door, and without waiting for permission, this tall, tanned-looking guy in a dark suit stepped in and started giving my room the once-over.

"Just a sec," I said to Merry. "Can I help you?"

If I didn't have such good manners, I would have said, "Excuse me, bud, but the party's downstairs."

"Just looking. Nice house."

He didn't look like the type who'd pull a knife on you, but, still, I didn't like having a strange guy hanging out in my room. He noticed that. "I'm in real estate," he said. "Houses." He pulled a card out of his pocket: "John Ely / Better Homes, Inc."

There was a sketch of a house in the corner and a phone number next to it.

"Thanks for the look," he said. "And you're . . . ?"

"Carter."

"Right," he said. "Your mother told me about you. Well, thanks, Carter. Be seeing ya."

He left, closing the door only partway behind him.

"Merry, you still there?"

"What was *that* about?"

"Some friend of my mom's just snooping around."

"Is he cute?"

"Maybe. Sort of. I don't know." He gave me the creeps. I didn't want to talk about him.

"So, are you disappointed?" Merry said.

I thought she was still talking about that guy. "Is it okay if we change the subject?"

"But I thought you were in such a rush to solve this case."

"I'm sorry," I said. "I got confused. Disappointed about what?"

"That the paints don't match up."

"Sure. But it's only one clue. Just because we haven't linked Judy and Corey to the paint doesn't mean they didn't do it. The fact still is that Judy paints, and she could have done it."

"True."

"Oh, God," I said.

"What's wrong?"

I held the phone away from my ear so she could

pick up the noise in the background. "Hear that?"
I asked.

"Barely. What is it?"

"That song."

"Oh noooo!"

The house was shaking with it. "Wild thing /
You make my heart sing . . ." They played it at
practically every party.

"Where did your mother get that record, anyway?"

"Supposedly it was a big hit when she was in
high school."

"Figures," Merry said. "Well, I should get ready
to go."

"What are you doing tonight?" I asked, even
though I didn't want to know what I was missing.

"Neil and I are going to the movies."

"Give my best to Mrs. Weinstein if you see her,"
I said.

"Yeah," Merry said. "Sure."

As soon as I put down the phone, it rang again.
It was Neil.

"Aren't you afraid your mother might pick up?"
I said.

"Don't worry, I've got something all worked
out, just in case. And, speaking of case . . . how's it
coming?"

I told him what Merry'd said about the paint,
that it was very expensive.

"Then you're looking for someone who's either
a serious painter or living with someone who is."

"Not necessarily," I said. "Someone could have gone out and bought the paint just for the occasion."

"No way. Who's going to buy twenty-dollar tubes of paint just to freak out Balboa? You'd use what you've got. Like in this book I read, there's a guy who wants to kill his landlady. Does he go out and buy a gun? No. He just uses an old ax he's got lying around."

"Does he kill her?"

"Yes, but he lives to regret it."

Someone picked up the phone. "Neil?" It was his mother. "Neil, who are you talking to?"

"Marko. We were just hanging up. 'Bye, Marko." And he hung up.

But just for a second. The phone rang again, and he was back, whispering. "Gotta make this quick," he said. "I did some checking, and Von Thelan's mother teaches art at the Adult Education Center. Her paint supply probably isn't bad."

CHAPTER 9

When I got up the next morning, I left my shades down so it wouldn't seem like Saturday. Even though I wasn't sure what I'd say, I started my piece about Balboa. I had already missed my deadline, but I knew if I turned it in on Monday, it could still make it into the next issue. I knew a lot of people would read it, because everyone was talking about what had been happening to Balboa.

Victim number one was found lying in the closet.

Victim number two had her body rattled by an electric charge.

Victim number three spent all night locked in an elevator.

What do victims one, two, and three have
   in common? They are all the same person: our biology teacher, Beverly Balboa.

That's as far as I'd gotten when the doorbell
rang. And rang again. One more ring, and I knew
who would be getting it: me.

It was Adrian, looking unhappy.

"I don't think Justin's up yet," I said. "But I'd
be glad to risk my life trying to wake him."

"I came to see *you*," she said. I looked at her
more closely. I could see she'd been crying.

I waved her in and we stood in the hallway
while she fished through her shoulder bag. "I know
your mom and Justin want you to quit investigating,
and I don't want you to get into trouble, but . . . this
came in the mail yesterday," she said, handing me
an envelope. It was addressed to her, only instead
of being typed or written, the address was spelled
out in letters cut from newspapers. It's an old trick —
so no one can trace the handwriting or the type-
writer model.

"Open it," she said.

Inside was a copy of the picture of her that had
appeared in the *St. Davids Tribune*.

But there was a difference between this picture
and the one I'd seen at her house. On the one her
mother had shown me, there wasn't a snake drawn
wrapped around her neck looking like it was going
to bite out her eyeball. On this one, there was.

And there was something else, at the bottom:

the words "Ambassadors of Doom," also spelled out in letters cut from a newspaper.

"It's a threat, isn't it?" she said.

"It isn't a valentine," I said. "But I wouldn't take it personally."

"Excuse me for saying so, Carter, but that doesn't make sense. This looks pretty personal to me." She held the picture in front of my face. It was hard to disagree.

Still, I tried to make her see it differently. "I don't think they have anything against *you* — it's what you represent that pisses them off — law, order, and school spirit. They're afraid the Ambassadors are going to ruin their fun, which right now is torturing Balboa."

She put the picture back into the envelope and gave it to me. "It gives me the creeps. You keep it. You'll probably need it for evidence anyway, right?"

"Adrian!" Justin was on the upstairs landing, his hair flying out from all sides. "I thought we'd said one o'clock."

"We did," she called up to him, in a much higher voice than she'd been using with me. I hate it when girls change their voices when a guy's around. It always sounds so phony to me, and I couldn't believe my own brother would fall for it. "But I have rehearsal later this afternoon, and a million things to do before then, so I was hoping we could get some work done now."

By the time she finished explaining, he'd come down to where we were standing.

"Okay," he said, "only, did you bring the dishes?"

"Got them right here," she said, reaching into her bag again, this time for four small glass disks.

"What are those?" I asked. I didn't care about finding out what the dishes were for as much as I wanted to remind them I was still there.

Justin answered. "Petri dishes."

"They're for my biology project," Adrian said. "You grow bacteria in them."

While she was talking, Justin looked at her closely. "Are you all right?"

"Sure," she said. "Why?"

"You look like you've been crying."

"I do?" She wiped at her eyes. "It must be from the cold. It's a little chilly outside." She wiped at the tears again, but they were still there when she pulled her hand away.

"I guess we should get to work, then," Justin said.

"I guess we should," Adrian agreed, following him toward the basement, where Justin's had a lab ever since he got a chemistry set for Christmas ten years ago. Before she disappeared downstairs, Adrian looked back at me and mouthed, "Thanks."

And I should have thanked her, too, or both of them, for letting me know what it's like to be invisible.

"This test will take the full class period," Balboa announced on Monday. She didn't look much better than she had when they pulled her from the elevator. Her skin was gray, like mushrooms. "Please clear all books and papers from your desk. You may begin as soon as you have your test."

She gave a stack of papers to the person at the head of each row, who passed them back. I took the last two from Dennis Erdman, and handed the very last one back to Linsey.

"Good luck," I said.

"Ha," was her response. I knew what she meant.

A balled-up gum wrapper hit me in the neck. I looked and saw Neil waiting to tell me something.

"Where's your boyfriend," he whispered.

Tony was absent. Findlay, too.

Neil raised one eyebrow and nodded — something he'd picked up from watching Humphrey Bogart movies on his parents' VCR.

I pretended to ignore him. But he was right. There was something strange about both of them missing the test.

The only sound in the room was the squish squash of Balboa's tennis shoes on the tile as she slowly limped her way up one aisle and down the other. I wished she wouldn't do that. It made me feel like she was grading us already. When she got to my aisle, she stood there so long I began to think I should invite her to sit and make herself at home.

But then she swooped and picked a sheet of paper off the books beside my desk. She was standing so close I could feel her start to shake. Next, she grabbed my arm and jerked me from my seat. With the whole class watching, she pulled me into the hall.

"What am I supposed to make of this?" Balboa waved the page in my face.

"What is it?"

"What is it?" she echoed me. "What *is* it? You tell *me* what it is." She thrust the paper under my nose. It was a copy of the test, with the answers filled in.

"How you thought you could get away with this . . ."

"But I —"

"Save it," she cut in, "for Mr. Musgrove." She handed me a hall pass, and, as if I couldn't walk it in my sleep by then, pointed the way to the office. "Stay until I get there."

"What now, Carter?" Musgrove barely looked up from his desk when I came in.

How do you tell someone who would probably blame you for everything from the assassination of Abraham Lincoln to the war in the Middle East that you've just been accused of something you didn't do?

"Mrs. Balboa sent me down," I explained, in the kind of voice I would use if I had to tell my mother I'd broken one of her precious crystal glasses. "We've had a misunderstanding."

He put his pen down, ran his hand over his face, and squinted at me, like the sun was right over my shoulder. "A misunderstanding?"

I told him what Balboa had found, and where. "But it isn't mine," I said. "And I didn't put it there."

"If it was next to *your* desk, on top of *your* books," he said, "whose is it and how did it get there?"

"That's what I'd like to know."

He set his elbows on the desk and lowered his head into his hands.

"I knew something was up when she offered to help me look for my keys," Mrs. Balboa said when she got to the office. "She *knew* where the keys were," she said, implying that I'd taken them, "so what she was really looking for was a copy of the test. And she found one." She laid the sheet in front of Musgrove.

I tried hard to remember she was a woman whose life had been marked by tragedy. But under the circumstances it wasn't easy.

"Well, Carter?" Musgrove looked at me.

He wanted me to confess. But, of course, I couldn't.

"This is ridiculous," Musgrove said. "You were caught red-handed, yet you deny it. Are you going to deny that you were in here going through the files the other night, too?"

"No," I said. "But this is different."

"I don't see that it's different at all. Only we're going to handle it differently, the way we should have handled it in the first place." He peeled a pink slip off a pad, filled in a few lines, then held it out to me. "You're suspended until your hearing," he said.

I took the slip and looked at Balboa, who wasn't

looking at me. I couldn't believe I was going through this for her benefit. I used to think that doing the right thing was always right. But suddenly I wasn't sure it was worth it. If I hadn't been trying to find out who was after Balboa, I wouldn't have been caught in the principal's office, which meant I wouldn't have been suspected of trapping Balboa in the elevator, which meant they probably wouldn't have been so quick to accuse me of cheating on the test.

But it was too late to quit. It wouldn't have been fair to stop just because I was pissed off at Balboa. Someone who would try to electrocute her and lock her in an elevator might be up for just about anything. Whatever happened next would probably be even worse.

There were two more reasons for staying on the case. I'd made a promise to Adrian, for one. And, last, but in no way least, to win out at my hearing, to keep from being expelled.

Adrian was outside the office, posting Linsey's picture on the Ambassador bulletin board. "You're not in trouble again!"

I told her about the cheat sheet.

"But who could have put it there? And why would someone do that to you?"

I told her those were good questions, and I had no idea.

"Maybe it belonged to someone else, who dropped it next to your desk by accident," she said.

"What if someone was relying on it to get through the test, then found it missing!" She laughed, and I had to smile, at that. Then she got serious.

"Is there anything I can do? What if I went in and stood up for you?" She nodded toward the office.

"Thanks." I considered it for a moment, then decided it wouldn't work. Musgrove is not the kind of guy who would let a student — any student — tell him he was wrong. "I don't think it would do any good. He's made up his mind."

"Okay," she said. "But if there's anything I can do . . ."

"You've been *what*?" Mom wasn't hysterical — yet. It was more like she couldn't believe it.

"Only until the hearing. And anyway, I'm not guilty. I didn't do it."

"Oh. Okay. Let me get this straight." She was being sarcastic now. "You've been suspended, but *only* until your hearing, at which time you are likely to be expelled. Is that the deal?"

"No. I'm not going to be expelled."

"How can you be so sure? You're in a lot of trouble." She was still calm. Stunned, I guess.

She went to the phone, opened the drawer in the telephone table, and pulled out a pack of cigarettes. I gave her the evil eye — she was supposed to have quit a few weeks ago. She gave me the eye right back.

"You have no right to be looking at me like that, missy. If it weren't for you, I wouldn't need to smoke." Once she'd lit one, she flipped through the phone book. Then she dialed.

She asked for Walter Musgrove.

While she waited she clicked her fingernails on the telephone table. Right next to where her fingers were tapping was a card like the one the real estate guy had given me: "John Ely / Better Homes, Inc."

I was just beginning to wonder what it meant that she kept a copy of his card by her phone, when Musgrove came on the line.

"How do you expect to maintain authority if you insist on suspending students without reasonable evidence?" Mom demanded.

She listened for a moment. "I know she's been in trouble before and I know she's not Little Miss Perfect. But I also know she would not cheat. That is simply something she would not do. Now, you either allow her back, or the next call you get will be from my lawyer."

She listened. "Yes, I am threatening you. But it's no less than you deserve for depriving my child of a fair hearing before you make a decision to kick her out of school. I will be sending her tomorrow, and if she shows up back here, you and the other addleheads who run this system will have a lot more to worry about than whether some kid's been cheating on her biology test."

She hung up without waiting for a reply. I didn't know whether to thank her or die of embarrassment.

"This town!" she shouted at the phone before turning to me.

"And *you!*" I wasn't prepared for that. "You act as if I have nothing to do but get you out of trouble. If you could bring yourself to stop being selfish for one minute you might realize I have a lot going on in my life right now, and I don't need another crisis."

I glanced at the card on the table and wondered if John Ely / Better Homes, Inc., was one of the things going on in her life.

"I'm sorry," I said, and meant it.

"You should be. You really should be."

"Excuse me, Carter, but I think you're being really dumb," Neil said when he called me from school. "You remind me of a case that made the papers a few years ago, where this woman lawyer fell in love with her client, who was accused of murder. She helped him escape, even though she knew he was guilty."

"But I don't *know* that Tony is guilty," I said.

"Your problem is that you won't even try to find out!" Neil shouted before lowering his voice. "Look," he said, "neither of them showed up for the test today."

"So?"

"So, that means they — or at least one of them — are afraid of failing."

"So?"

"If you know a teacher is going to fail you, she's not going to be your favorite teacher. And don't forget the 'no pass, no play' rule. We've been through this before."

"But just because she's not your favorite teacher, you're not necessarily going to lock her in an elevator . . ."

"*You* might not, and *I* might not, but two guys together, who have been known to get each other to do some wild things — they just *might*."

"Maybe . . ."

"Look, I know you're in love with the guy —"

"I am not 'in love' with him!"

"You don't have to kid me, Carter. I know. But would you listen, please?" He paused. "I know you're in love with him, but if you're serious about solving this case, you'd better get your priorities straight."

I was furious at him — because I knew he was right. I didn't like it, but there were reasons to suspect Von Findlay. And even though I preferred to suspect Judy and Corey, they were reasons I had to investigate. Later that afternoon, I did.

The lawn at Findlay's house was growing out like a bad haircut. There were two junked cars in the front yard; it looked like they'd been dropped there by giant birds. I leaned my bike against one of them.

The house looked just as dead as the cars: the paint was falling off in big chips so the front was like a jigsaw puzzle with pieces missing. The doorbell rattled hopelessly in its socket, so I knocked.

Then I panicked. I'd forgotten to think of something to say. I couldn't give my real reason for being there — to find out if Findlay had skipped school. I prayed for no one to be home.

But someone was. He swung the door open, then rested on the knob while he waited for me to explain myself. He was a pint-sized version of Peter, wearing a T-shirt torn at the shoulder with the sleeve barely holding on. I could hear enough of the television from where I stood to know the show he was watching involved a lot of bullets.

"Is Peter home?" I asked.

"No."

"Do you know where he is?"

"No."

"Do you know when he'll be back?"

"No."

"Do you think he's at Tony's?"

"Maybe."

"Well, thanks a lot." Yeah, thanks a lot.

He didn't tell me much, but it wasn't a total waste. I learned something: Peter Findlay was not at home sick.

I used to think a lot about what it would be like to go to Tony's house. But I never thought it would be the way it was that day. I'm too embarrassed to admit what I had imagined, but it certainly wasn't creeping up on the house to look for evidence that he was terrorizing a teacher.

Except for the junked car in the driveway, Von Thelan's house was nothing like Findlay's. Their similarities had to stop somewhere, I guess.

From the way the yard was fixed up you'd expect a big house. Someone had planted patches of flowers and set up birdbaths — three of them. But the house was one of those mobile homes with the wheels gone. There was rust around the bottom that made it look like it had been there for a long time.

I left my bike by the car and went to the door feeling like someone was inside my heart with a hammer. Pound — I hope he's here. Pound — I hope he's not.

He wasn't home. No one was. The hammering stopped.

I looked around the place, not because I expected to find anything having to do with Balboa, but just to be there, where Tony started out and ended up each day.

The backyard looked like the floor of a hardware store after a tornado: nails, tools, electrical cords everywhere. The piles of hardware were more organized the closer I got to the car, which was almost sliding off the cinder blocks that were supposed to be holding it up.

There was a garage behind the car and I went over and stuck my face against the window. Someone was using it as a bedroom; from the lacrosse posters on the wall, I guessed it was Tony. I held my hands up to cut the glare, and got as good a look at his room as I could through my own reflection and the streaks of dirt on the glass.

"Kind of a mess, huh?" The voice bonked me like a block of wood. Tony was standing behind me with his arms folded. "If I'd known you were coming, I would've cleaned up."

"I thought I saw my dog run into your yard," I said, as if that would explain why I was looking into his bedroom window.

"What kind of dog?"

I hadn't thought of that. ". . . A small one."

"Like what kind?" he asked. "Poodle, schnauzer, dachshund . . ."

"Mutt. A small black furry mutt. Looks more like a cat."

I wanted to die. Next best thing — I headed back to my bike.

"I'll let you know if I see it," he said. "What's its name, just in case?"

Another thing I hadn't thought of. "Fido," I said. Then I got inspired. "I was going to name it Balboa, since she's such a dog. But then I didn't think it would be fair to do that to a harmless pet." I waited for his reaction, but there wasn't much.

"Yeah," he said. "Did you take that test today?"

"I took more of it than you and Peter did," I said.

He looked at his shoes, and for a second I thought he was going to cry. "We had an accident. Peter's at St. Davids. I was there with him most of the day." St. Davids Hospital.

"What happened?"

He nodded back toward the garage. "We were working on the car this morning and one of the cinder blocks broke. The car dropped" — he made a sound meant to be a falling automobile — "and crushed his arm."

"Is he going to be okay?" I said. "What about lacrosse?"

"They didn't know." He really did look like he was going to cry. I wished Neil could have been there. Then he'd know this was not the kind of guy to go around locking teachers in elevators.

I waited to see if he'd say anything else, but he seemed to be waiting for me to go. I got on my bike.

"I'll let you know if I find him," he said.

"Find who?"

"Your *dog*."

I pulled away, and right when I was telling myself what a jerk I was, I saw something that made me feel even worse.

Judy Mancini was going up to Tony's house, and he was at the door, waiting for her.

CHAPTER 10

"You really think he likes her?" Merry was on the phone, trying to think of another explanation for Judy being at Tony's.

"Why else would she be there?" I asked.

"*You* were there and he doesn't like you," she said.

"Thanks a lot."

"Anyway, doesn't this make your case easier? If Tony and Judy are going together, they might be going after Balboa together, too. So instead of having all these separate suspects, you just have one group."

"I'd rather have Tony," I said.

"Why would you want the kind of guy who'd like Judy? If he likes someone like *her,* he's not the guy for you."

I thought about the things we'd seen Judy do

in the mall and tried to agree. "Maybe you're right. And that story about Peter's arm . . . even if it's true, why were they working on the car instead of going to school?"

"Good point," she said.

"Can I ask you a favor?"

"What now?"

"Please don't tell Neil that I suspect Tony. I feel stupid changing my mind like this."

"I'm sure he'll understand if you tell him," she said. "Remember, it's his business, too, since he might get expelled along with you."

"I know. But please? Once I get the case solved, then he'll know."

"Okay," she said. "See you tomorrow."

I left for school early the next day, planning to find Balboa. I thought if I could talk to her alone I might be able to convince her someone else was behind the "pranks."

Balboa was at her desk, going over a stack of papers — the tests from the day before. When my shoes clacked on the tile, she gasped and her head jerked up.

"What are you doing here?" She looked embarrassed that I'd frightened her.

"I just wanted to tell you I'm sorry for everything you've been through . . ."

She looked at me like she was expecting me to spring something on her any second.

"And that I didn't do any of it — the elevator or the cheating thing."

"So you've said before," she said.

I felt like she *wanted* me to be guilty. Maybe if I let her know I cared about her —

"I was using some old newspapers to do my homework the other night," I said, "and I read about your car accident . . ."

She stared at me, and for once I couldn't tell what the look was saying. She didn't seem angry and she didn't necessarily seem *not* angry. "It made me feel twice as bad about what's been happening," I said.

She kept staring at me, and then I knew I shouldn't have brought it up. I should have known I wouldn't get anything from her.

"Carter," she said, putting down her pencil, "I would like to believe you. But it's hard for me to know what else to think. One thing I've learned from detective novels is to look for a culprit who has a motive and an opportunity. Without going over the details, I think it's fair to say that you have both."

"You read detective novels?" It was too much to believe I had something in common with Balboa.

She smiled, like I'd discovered a secret she wasn't especially proud of.

"Ever read Ross Macdonald?"

"*Underground Man* is one of my favorites," she said. "And now, if you'll excuse me." She picked up her pencil and that was it. She went back to work.

Von Findlay showed up for school the next day. Peter's arm was in a cast and his mouth was going a mile a minute telling everyone what'd happened. It killed me to look at Tony. Why hadn't I noticed about him and Judy before? Simple — because it looked like he spent all his time with Peter. And she seemed to hang out with no one but Corey. Even now that I knew about them, it was hard to see it. They didn't walk each other to class or pass notes or do any of the usual couple things.

I ran into Musgrove once during the day. But he didn't say anything to me about Mom's phone call.

"You didn't happen to see Adrian on the way home," Justin said first thing when I got in the door.

"No. She supposed to be here?"

"Yeah," he said. "She's only a few minutes late. It's okay."

Only it didn't sound like he thought it was okay.

"When was she supposed to be here?"

"Around four."

I looked at my watch. It was about five thirty. I told him.

"It's okay," he said again.

It *wasn't* okay. Adrian had come over early last weekend and expected Justin to hop out of bed to help her. And now, when he was expecting her, she just didn't show up.

"Why does she need you to help her with that project anyway?" I asked. "She's supposed to be so smart."

"She *is* smart," Justin said. "She just has trouble in science. A lot of people who are good in other subjects have a hard time with science. And vice versa."

"But the only reason she asked *you* is because she had a crush on you, not because she really cared about doing better in biology."

"That's not true," he said, in a way that made me feel like I was being unfair. "She picked me because she knew that I understand Mrs. Balboa and the kind of work she expects."

Mom called from upstairs. "Carter, do me a favor and vacuum the front hall. Someone's coming over and I don't want the place looking like a pigsty."

I was rolling the vacuum out of the front closet when Justin's prayers were answered: Adrian showed.

"He's downstairs," I said, although I wanted to say more, about how unfair it was for her to keep him waiting. But I had this feeling she might convince me there was a good reason for it. And maybe, after all, there was.

She thanked me and headed down.

I ran the vacuum and when I stopped, the doorbell was ringing. It might have been ringing the whole time for all I knew — because when I got to the door, the guy was turning to leave. He turned back when he heard me.

It was John Ely / Better Homes, Inc.

"Well, hi there. Glad to see someone's home."

He was talking so loud you'd think I was across the room instead of right in front of him. And the way he was dressed up in this suit and bright red tie, you could tell he thought he was something special, which I would have been glad to tell him he was not.

"Is your mother here?" He winked when he said it. "We've got a date to go over some wallpaper samples." He held up a fat album.

"She's upstairs," I said. Before I could ask him to wait, he said, "Great," and walked right past me into the hall. I hadn't rolled the vacuum away yet, and I was hoping he'd trip over it. But he managed not to.

"I'll get her," I said. I went upstairs and told Mom "he" was here. She left and I picked up the phone. Having this guy in the house made me miss Art.

"Can't take your call right now . . ."

This time I left a message. "Daddy, it's me. I want to talk to you. I don't care how late you get this message. Please call me."

I went to my room, finished my piece about Balboa, then went to bed. Art didn't call.

The next morning, I dropped my piece in the "press" box and ran off before Sheila could get on me for being late.

While I was making my getaway, Neil cornered me in the hall. "You're avoiding me," he said.

"I don't want to get you in trouble with your mom," I answered.

"At school? Come on. I know the reason. It's because of what I said about your boyfriend."

"He is not my boyfriend, and you're going to make me late for class." Normally, next period would have been study hall, but I had to spend it taking the makeup exam for Balboa.

"Whoa. Hold on there, Carter," Musgrove called as I charged by his door. "Let me see you a minute."

It was like déjà vu. Again Donny Gillespie was on his way out. I was going to have to stop thinking of Donny as a delinquent, unless I was willing to think of myself that way, too. After all, we spent about the same amount of time in Musgrove's office.

Once Donny had cleared the door, Musgrove handed my article about Balboa back to me.

"First, you should know, students who are in trouble for any reason — grades or conduct — cannot participate in extracurricular activities. That means you're off the paper until your hearing."

That's why Sheila hadn't come after me for the pieces. She knew about the rule.

"But even if you were allowed on the paper staff, I would never let this piece run. This is the most irresponsible 'article' I've ever seen," he said. "Who are *you* to be flinging accusations at other students? Besides, you have no proof that" — he grabbed the story back from me and read from it — " 'there is a group of students deliberately harassing Mrs. Balboa and threatening her safety.' " He put the story down. "That kind of speculation is dangerous. You might give people ideas. Maybe that's what you want. Do you think you'll get yourself off the hook that way? By encouraging the kind of behavior that got you into trouble? 'Gee,' " he said, like he was mimicking me, " 'maybe if everyone starts doing it, I won't look so bad.' "

"But what about what you said in the p.a. announcement last week? You said something was up something that had to be stopped."

"I am the principal."

I wanted to ask what difference that made, but something in his look warned me against it. My only hope remained to solve the case.

Tony was surprised to see me when I showed for the makeup exam. "I thought you took the test," he said, leaning toward me.

"It's a long story," I replied, trying hard to remember that this guy liked Judy and was possibly a dangerous psycho.

"You can tell me later," he said.

Later. Maybe I could save him from the life of trouble Judy would lead him into.

We didn't have to go anywhere after the test, because biology class was next. Nothing awful happened during class — not until the final bell rang, and I realized my period had started.

I bolted for the bathroom and discovered, of course, that I didn't have a pad or a tampon with me. And, of course, the machine was empty. I was sitting on the toilet thinking that the only thing I could do was wait until someone else came along and borrow one from her. Borrow isn't exactly the word — it isn't something you'd ever return.

Then the fire alarm went off. Great timing for a drill.

I decided to sit it out where I was. I stretched my feet in front of me, just in case someone checked in to see if anyone was hiding in the girls' room.

I heard everyone charging out of the building while I sat reading the graffiti on the stall. "Musgrove Sucks," "Wayne loves Laurel," and underneath that, "Laurel loves Greg."

And then, in small letters, just like the ones in the elevator: "Ambassadors of Doom."

Whoever wrote "Balboa Beware" on the elevator had been in the girls' room.

I was one clue closer to Judy and Corey.

The alarm clanged on and on — longer than any drill I'd been in before. Then came a smell telling me why: it wasn't a drill. It was smoke. Serious something's-burning smoke. The school was on fire.

I stuffed toilet paper into my underpants. It would have to do. I wasn't going to get burned alive just because I didn't have a tampon. A period's bad enough without having to die because of it.

The hall stank, like eggs you keep around too long after Easter. The fumes made me dizzy, so I held my breath and ran for it.

Everyone had cleared out, except for three people still heading down the stairs. Balboa was one. Judy and Corey were the others. Each had an arm around Balboa.

I froze, watching. Waiting. Were they going to push her? Let her fall?

Neither. They walked her all the way out.

It was like a nightmare out there. The smoke made it look like there was a storm coming, and paramedics were running around clapping masks over as many faces as they could, Merry's included. She looked like a prehistoric insect.

"Mer! Are you okay?" Merry nodded, then pressed her palm against her forehead; the nod had made her dizzy. "What happened?"

She pointed at the school, at smoke spilling from an open window. Balboa's window. She pulled the mask away for a second. "Something blew up." She let the mask snap back down, then pulled it out to talk again. "Is Mrs. Balboa all right?"

I nodded. I must not have looked too thrilled because Merry asked, "Aren't you glad?"

Of course I wasn't glad. It *was* good she didn't get hurt, but I wasn't glad that Judy and Corey had been the ones to save her. Who was I going to suspect now?

"How did it happen?" I asked.

Merry lifted the mask again. "I was getting up to change class. Then *Bang! Whoosh!*" — she held her head again — "there was this puddle of fire by Balboa's desk." She paused. "Something's bugging you."

I told her about Judy and Corey.

"That's too bad," Neil said. He'd been standing right behind me.

"Did *you* see what happened?" I asked him.

"Nope. I was already at the door. The juniors were going in."

"Your friend is not supposed to be talking." The paramedic meant Merry, and he was speaking to me and Neil. He was a lumpy guy, with curly hair and goofy eyes that looked like wobbly blue balls. "Think you can walk to the van?" he asked Merry, pointing to the red-and-white ambulance a few steps away.

"You're not taking her to the hospital!" I said.

"It's routine. Something we do whenever someone's been exposed to toxic fumes. Chances are she's fine."

"Call me later," I said to Merry. "Tell me how it goes."

Neil reached to put his arm around me — to comfort me, I guess. But I got out of it. I had work to do.

I went to Judy and asked her if she'd seen how the fire started. "Nope," she said.

It was strange to be talking right to her after all the time I'd spent listening in on her conversations.

"Yeah," Corey said, "we never pay attention in class."

"It's sort of a wonder we even paid attention to the fire," Judy said.

"Anything to get out of school," Corey added.

"But you took your time getting out," I said. "You helped Balboa."

"Look." Judy was on the verge of cracking up. "Everyone makes mistakes."

"We figured maybe she couldn't flunk us if we saved her life," Corey said. "God, Jude, what are you going to do about your purse?"

"I guess there isn't much I can do about it now."

"You left your purse in there?" I asked.

"Yeah. I got up to help Balboa and didn't get a chance to go back and grab it."

That about settled it. If Judy hated Balboa enough to do what I suspected her of doing, she wouldn't have sacrificed her purse to save the teacher.

Musgrove stood on the school steps to make an announcement. Sweat was raining down his face, and his shirt was soaked from his armpits to his belt.

School was closed for the day, he said. And because of toxic fumes no one would be let back into the building for any reason.

Everyone cheered. Everyone but me. I *had* to get back in there, to look for clues.

Donny Gillespie was hanging around, replaying the fire with a couple of guys. "Did you hear Winnie Myers? 'Oh my God! Oh my God! Oh, Mrs. Balboa, my God!' "

"And did you see Balboa's face when she saw it?" Wayne Davis said, scrunching up his eyes and nose like he smelled smoke, then dropping his jaw in panic.

"She about froze, man," Michael D. observed. "Froze when she saw that fire, man."

"I don't blame her," Wayne said. "How'd you like to have your ass slip on the floor, then be damn near electrocuted, then stuck in an elevator, then damn near burned alive?"

And things were only going to get worse.

I took my time about butting into their conversation. Those guys always make me feel like they're imagining what I look like without my clothes.

"So," I said. "What happened in there?"

"I don't know. Must've been someone doing something, though," Wayne said.

"Anyone you know?"

"Might have been," Donny said, lighting a match and letting it burn down to his fingers.

"I think it was Davis here, myself," Michael D. said.

"And I think it was Michael D.," Wayne said.

"What would you do if you knew?" Donny asked.

"Nothing," I said. "Just curious."

"Would you go out with me if I tell you who it was?" Wayne asked.

"Leave my girl alone." Michael D. grabbed Wayne's arm and twisted it. "I've been in love with her longer than you." I left before they could embarrass me any more.

"Carter Colborn!" Mr. Herlihy was waving his arms at me. "I have something might help you."

He held out his clenched fist, then slowly opened his hand. Inside was a matchbook. A clump of matches was missing. "It was in the lab. Right near where the fire started," he said. "I picked it up because I thought it might be the kind of thing you would be looking for."

I took it from him. "You're right. This is what I'd look for."

"You think you can use it, then?"

I read the name of the place on the matchbook. Pedroni Pizza. Yes, I could use it.

CHAPTER 11

I got on my bike and went after Neil. I caught up with him just before he turned onto his block, which, thanks to Mrs. Weinstein, was out of bounds for me. We planned to meet at Pedroni's that night, and not because either one of us had a craving for pizza. I wanted to see who else would show. Whoever had used Pedroni's matches to torch Balboa's classroom might hang out there.

"You didn't happen to see Adrian after the fire," Justin said while I was getting ready to go.

"No. Why?"

"I thought she might come over since we got out early, but I haven't heard from her. There couldn't be any play rehearsal, with the school closed."

"Did you call her house?"

He nodded. "Her mother thought she might be here."

Thinking of Merry, I asked, "Have you tried the hospital?"

He nodded again. "She's not there, either."

Thinking of Tony and Judy, I asked, "Do you think she's seeing someone else?"

From the way he looked at me, I could tell the idea had never crossed his mind.

"Want me to investigate?"

"No," he said. "I don't think that's it. She's probably busy with drama club. The play's opening in a few days."

"You give her all the breaks in the world, and she's so rude to you. You're practically doing her biology project for her — the least she could do is show up on time."

He got angry. "What do you have against her all of a sudden?"

I really couldn't say. Maybe it was jealousy — Justin wasn't spending as much time with me as he used to. Or maybe I was mad at her for taking advantage of him. Or maybe, and most likely, it was a little bit of both.

Pedroni's was packed, and Neil and I had to wait to get the right table.

"I can seat you now if you want to take that booth over there," the hostess said. It was getting to be a strain on her, trying to be polite to two high school kids who'd already turned down three tables.

"No, thank you. We'll wait for one of those," I said, pointing to three tables in the corner — each of them occupied. She shrugged, and led the couple behind us to the empty booth.

Neil pulled a crumpled receipt from his pocket and started writing on the back. "I read this story once," he said. "A true story about a guy who had a tape recorder going in his pocket while he was being murdered. He got killed. But he also got the name of the killer, the motive, and the way it was done."

He showed me what he'd been writing: "Carter Colborn starved me to death." Then he folded it and tucked it back into his pocket. "Now when they find my corpse lying here," he said, patting the pocket with the note, "there won't be any mystery."

But he knew there wasn't any point to being there unless we sat where we could see everyone who came and went. We had to wait for a table with a view. There were only three of them.

I watched the people at the tables we wanted. One couple would be there all night; they were having a fight. No one, no matter how mad they were at each other, would leave a Pedroni pizza, so I figured they still had to finish their argument, make up, then get through the medium-size double cheese cooling between them.

Then there was another couple, with a two-year-old who was celebrating his first pizza. Dad was taking pictures of the kid sticking his hand into a slice and stretching the cheese out like a rubber band. They'd be a while, too.

Then there was the third couple. They were so

glued to each other it was just luck I got the woman to see I was staring at her. It was a technique I'd learned from Art, who hates to wait in restaurants. He calls it "staring 'em out," and it involves fixing the evil eye on whoever's at a table you want.

Once she saw the look I gave her, she couldn't get back into it with her boyfriend. She nudged him to get the check.

It was rude to ruin her evening; but they had finished their pizza, and I had serious business. Somebody's life was at stake.

"We are not going to fight over what we want on this pizza," Neil said once we'd sat down.

"Of course we're not. We're going to get exactly what I want."

"You're starting in —"

"Okay, what do you want?"

"Extra cheese, mushrooms, pepperoni."

"And anchovies," I said.

"What?"

"Anchovies. It's fair. I *hate* pepperoni. I'll need the anchovies to hide the taste."

"Like I said, we're not going to fight. I'll relinquish the pepperoni if you'll concede on the anchovies."

"Fair enough."

"Now," Neil said, leaning toward me, "we get to fight about something more important. Von Findlay."

"When are you going to get off that?" I asked. I still didn't want to tell him I suspected them, too.

"After the fire, they are more suspicious than ever," he said.

"And why is that?"

"I was hoping you would ask." He slumped down so he could fish around in his pocket. He pulled out two pieces of paper. One was the note he'd written while we waited. The other was a drawing of the biology lab. "Here," he said, pointing to a spot in front of Balboa's desk, "is where the fire started. And here" — he pointed to the desk — "is where she piled the test papers."

"They wanted to burn up the exams?"

"Precisely," he said, pulling the drawing away and looking disgustingly pleased with himself.

"If they show up here, I may start to believe you," I said, although he'd made a good point. A point I couldn't ignore.

I looked around for possible suspects. All I saw were either college couples or parents with kids. No one even vaguely familiar.

Until Musgrove walked in.

He acted like he owned the place — greeting the waitresses, slapping the busboys on the back, and heading toward the take-out counter, then out of view.

I was just getting up to follow him when the waitress came for our order, blocking my way.

We ordered, then I went after Musgrove.

The take-out counter was so busy no one noticed when I slid behind it, past the "business office," into the kitchen.

The place was huge, almost as big as the dining room. Pots hung from racks running along the wall and ceiling. Pizza pans, bright as mirrors, were stacked on a counter where this burly guy with the hairiest arms I've seen outside a zoo was pounding, slapping, and tossing dough like he had something serious against it.

Another guy, less hairy but just as big, was ladling sauce onto pizzas. Then he'd check the order slip and toss other ingredients on top. He'd wipe his hands on his apron, then slide the pizza into the oven like he was playing shuffleboard.

There were a few other guys, chopping, and emptying bins of dirty dishes into a sink the size of a bathtub. But no Musgrove.

I was about to ask around, when a trash barrel walked in through the back door. A walking trash barrel with smoke puffing from the top. When it stopped moving, I saw what was going on: the guy carrying the barrel wasn't much taller than it. And he was smoking a cigarette.

It was Donny Gillespie.

"You haven't seen Musgrove here tonight, have you?" I said.

"Yeah. He was here. Like just about every night lately."

"Every night?"

"The man likes pizza, okay?"

"I guess. But every night?"

"Maybe not every night. But five times a week." The cigarette had burned down almost to his lips.

He dropped it onto the floor, ground it with his foot, and fished in his shirt pocket for another. He scrunched his face as he lit it. With Pedroni Pizza matches.

"Why do you care if he hangs out here? You hot for him or something?"

"Give me a break . . ."

"I dunno. Seems like you'd get enough of him at school without following him around town."

"I have to ask him something, and I thought you could tell me where he went."

"He was here. Where he went . . . can't help you."

But he had helped me a lot. By being there. By lighting that cigarette with those matches. By getting touchy when I mentioned Musgrove.

I looked around once more. No Musgrove.

The pizza had arrived by the time I got back to Neil, who hadn't touched it. "I was waiting for you," he said, and reached in for a slice.

"I know who it is," I said. He stopped in mid-bite, waiting to hear.

"Musgrove and Donny are in it together."

He bit, and chewed. "Wake up, Carter. That's the dumbest idea you've had yet."

"No, it makes sense," I said. "Donny's doing lousy in school — he has at *least* as much against Balboa as Von Findlay. And either he or Musgrove has been at the scene of each of the crimes. And Donny works here and uses Pedroni matches."

"And what does Musgrove get from this?"

"The principal job. He wants it, but Balboa has a better chance. If he gets her out of the way . . . he's in."

"You don't think he plans to *kill* her —"

"No, just shake her up enough to make her think she might be better off, I don't know, selling insurance or" — I pointed to a waitress about Balboa's age — "serving pizza."

"What makes you think they're in it together?"

"Musgrove is here tonight. He went back there, where Donny works. But Donny says he doesn't know where he is. He was covering up for him. Plus," I said, "Donny's been spending a lot of time in the principal's office."

"You would know," Neil said.

"And a few more things. Donny is probably the worst delinquent in school — you know how he's always fighting. I didn't screw up half as bad as he does, and look who Musgrove wants to kick out. I think Musgrove's giving him a special deal to be his Ambassador of Doom.

"*Plus* Musgrove didn't let my story run in the paper. I think it's because he doesn't want people investigating. He's afraid he'll get caught. *And* the biology exam. I'll bet he had Donny plant it there so he'd have an excuse to suspend me and get me off the case."

"I don't know, Carter —"

"Oh my God," I said, watching Musgrove move from the kitchen area to the front door.

"There he is," Neil said.

"He was back there the whole time. I'll bet he saw me. I'll bet Donny knew exactly where he was."

"What's next?"

"Stakeout at Musgrove's house."

Neil shook his head. "If you ask me, you're making things hard on yourself. If you'd only face facts and admit it's Von Findlay . . ."

I took a slice. "But I *didn't* ask you," I said.

I nudged Neil on the way out. "Who does it look like in that car over there?"

"Which car?"

"The Pedroni delivery car. We just walked past it."

He looked over his shoulder. "The tall skinny guy looks like Bob Earle. The frizzed-out blonde looks like Adrian."

"That's what I thought. Wait here." I left him while I crept next to the Honda parked behind the delivery car. I crouched there to watch and listen. Their windows were down, but the wind was blowing their words away from me.

Bob was using his hands a lot. He was upset. Adrian kept edging closer to him. Trying to calm him down? Finally, she reached out and smoothed his hair. Then he leaned toward her. They kissed.

My stomach twinged like someone was pinching it with a clothespin. Justin didn't deserve this.

A car door slammed, and Adrian's heels were clicking my way. I had failed to notice that the car I was crouching next to was hers.

"Carter! You scared me!" she said.

"Sorry." I didn't know what to say next, but I said something anyhow. "Neil and I were walking by and I thought I'd stop and say hello . . ."

"I was helping Bob make some deliveries. . . . He just started this job." She paused. "How long have you been here?"

"A few minutes," I said.

"Then," she said, lowering her head, "you saw us?" She meant the kiss.

I nodded.

"It's hard for me to explain, but I'll try if you'll listen."

I nodded again.

"First of all, I consider Justin my boyfriend. He's the only guy I really like. Bob is someone who's been a friend for a long time. But he wants to be more than a friend and I've been too chicken to tell him no."

"Chicken?"

"I'm afraid he'll get mad at me and I won't have him as a friend anymore."

"But doesn't he know about Justin? Everyone else does."

"Yes," she said. "But he's hoping I'll break up with him."

"And you haven't said you're not going to?"

"Of course I have! But he won't listen. And I haven't forced the issue because, like I said, I want him as a friend."

"Justin worries about you. Whenever you're late, he thinks you might have had an accident."

"I know. And I'm really sorry. Justin is the best, and it'd kill me if he broke up with me."

I decided I wouldn't tell Justin what I'd seen. But I wasn't going to tell her that. Let her squirm.

"Can I drop you at your house? I should have been there a while ago. At this rate, my biology project will never get done."

I called for Neil, and we climbed into the car.

"How's your project coming?" I asked once we were on our way.

"You'll have to ask your brother," Adrian said. "He knows what's supposed to be happening with it — I just do what he says."

"What's it on?" Neil asked.

"Bacteria. I'm growing it in petri dishes."

"What are you going to do with them? Start an epidemic?" Neil said.

"What a sick idea!" Adrian said. "By the way, Carter, I meant to invite you to the meeting at my house Saturday morning."

"What meeting?"

"Remember what I said about improving student-faculty relations? The drama club is giving a preview performance of *Guys and Dolls* on Sunday, just for the faculty and the graduating Ambassadors, with a special dinner beforehand. The Ambassadors are fixing the dinner. And I'd like you to help out. If you want."

How obvious can you get? She was just inviting me to make me "forget" what I'd seen. Still, hanging out with the Ambassadors might help my reputation with the faculty. I said I'd go.

The next day I wanted to go straight from school to stake out Musgrove's. But it wasn't going to work. I was grounded, and had to go straight home instead.

I'd been there under an hour when the doorbell rang and John Ely was back, asking for Mom, who came up behind me to tell him she'd be ready in a second.

"They'll be coming with the paint for the porch tomorrow," he shouted after her.

"Who? Why?" I asked. No one had told me anything about painting the porch.

He winked. "Don't you think it's about ready for a fresh coat? And wait'll you see the color we picked out." Mom returned with a sweater and her purse.

"I'll be back around ten. And remember. No friends in the house."

I wasn't thrilled that she was going off with him, but I was glad she was going. I raced for my bike and was on my way to Musgrove's.

Musgrove lived in the Victoria Garden Apartments, a two-story brick building around a courtyard. In California, there would've been a pool in the center, but in Pennsylvania, where everyone's too much of a prude to splash around in swimsuits in front of everyone else, there were only trees and shrubs, and a big Dempsey dumpster. There was also a bike rack, where I locked mine up.

I looked over the names on the mailboxes to see if anyone I knew lived there. It would've made things easier if I'd had another apartment to watch him from. No such luck. But an empty apartment would work just as well, and there was a mailbox with no name on it. Apartment 7-B. I headed up to check it out.

A month's worth of advertising circulars were piled at the door, and a crack in the curtains showed an empty room. It was clear no one was living there. Not that it would do me much good — the door was probably locked. I tried it. Lo and behold, it opened.

I went in and locked the door behind me.

Just in time, too. From the window I could see Musgrove getting home from the supermarket. He made three trips to his car and back, carrying three bags of groceries each time. No wonder he was so fat. That was a lot of food for one guy.

But then I saw it wasn't just for him. He had a roommate. And not the kind you might expect. She was slender, with long, wet hair, and, like she'd just come out of the shower, she was wearing a bathrobe that wasn't belted tightly enough.

She came to the door and took one of the bags from him and he leaned down to kiss her. The way he kissed her, I could tell this was not his sister visiting from out of town. This was not his cousin or his niece. This was "a woman."

They disappeared for a few minutes, and when they showed again, she was wearing jeans and a big shirt, and they were hauling boxes of trash through the courtyard to the dumpster.

Then I heard the doorknob rattle. "That's funny" — it was an old woman's voice — "I'm sure

I left it unlocked." There was a click. It was unlocked now. And she was coming in. "I think you'll like it." She wasn't alone. "It's spacious."

The closet, I thought. But no. If she's showing the apartment, the customer will want to see the storage space. The back door? No, I'd have to run right in their path. There was no place to go.

"Do I know you?" the landlady asked.

"I don't think so."

"Then what are you doing in my apartment?"

"I was looking around. A friend and I are looking for a place like this."

The customer, a tall, weedy college type, didn't buy my story. "How old are you?"

"I'm younger than most people who get their own apartment, if that's what you're getting at."

"Yeah," he said.

"If you're interested in an apartment," the landlady said, "make an appointment through me. Otherwise you are trespassing, and I would have to call the police."

"I understand. Thank you." I edged out the door before the idea of calling the cops had time to grow on her.

Art says you can tell a lot about people from their garbage. You can tell where they do their shopping and how much they spend (check the receipts), what they eat, who they owe money to (look at return addresses on envelopes), and other things — some too gross to mention. With that in mind, I headed for the dumpster.

The most important thing was what I didn't

find. Not a single Pedroni Pizza box. If he was taking out from there night after night after night, like Donny said, there'd be box after box after box.

I spent the next hour hanging out in the parking lot right behind the apartment so I could duck behind a car if I saw him coming. The waiting was a good reminder of why I don't want to be a detective for a living. Most of it isn't as exciting as they make it on TV. Most of it is waiting for suspects to do something suspicious.

Eventually *she* came out again with another load of trash. She pushed the door wide and the cooking smells that came out with her reminded me it was past dinnertime, and I was starving.

When she went back in, the smells hit me again. She opened a window, and through it I heard her yell, "Smells wonderful, Bunny. Think you'll have everything ready in time?"

Bunny?

"What time did you invite them for?" he yelled somewhere in the background. "You told me, but I forgot."

"Eight."

I checked my watch and figured I wouldn't miss much if I rode to the mall for some food before their guests arrived. By the time I got back, there were more cars to hide behind. Spying would be easier.

The guests showed up in clumps. Maybe they were *her* friends. That would explain why there were so many. It was hard to imagine there were that many people in the world who liked Musgrove.

But I was wrong. Everyone slapped him on the back or hugged him when he met them at the door. I crept a few cars closer so I could hear what they were saying.

"Congratulations, Walt," a guest said. "You'll make a hit of it. I know it."

"Whoa," Musgrove said. "It's not mine yet."

"But I thought this was supposed to be a victory celebration!"

"It was — and it still may be. But I've hit a snag. I expect to know before long, one way or another."

Were they talking about the principal job? Was that what they meant? Of course. What else would Musgrove have to celebrate? His friends thought he had the job in the bag. But Balboa was still around. *She* was the snag. She was still in the running.

And I had to warn her before Musgrove put her out of it.

CHAPTER 12

I rode off to see Balboa.

But then I got that sinking feeling in my stomach, like when you've spent half your life on an algebra problem and you're sure you've got it until you realize you don't. There were clues that didn't fit with Musgrove. Like the handwriting in the girls' room, and Judy being at Tony's, and Tony being with Peter, who is in chronic trouble with Balboa.

When I got to her street, I knew it wasn't time to tell her anything. I had nothing to tell.

Since I was on her road, I decided to take it to where it joined the street leading back to my house. It was a narrow road, and so shaded by trees it was more like a path through the woods. It twisted and turned so much I had to ride slowly to keep from going off it — like the Dodge Dart ahead of me that'd swerved into a clump of bushes.

As far as I knew, only one person in St. Davids drove a white Dodge Dart: Balboa.

I got off my bike and looked the car over. I felt the hood — it was still warm. Everything looked fine, except the right rear tire, which was hanging there like a doughnut leaning against a coffee cup. I bent to look at it, and the ground began to rattle — a tow truck was coming.

Good thing it was dark — too dark for the driver to see me under there. I crept back to my bike as he stopped the truck under a streetlight. I memorized the service station name and phone number written on the door, and just as I was about to ride away, an all-too-familiar voice hit me from behind. "Hello there!" I froze with my fingers on the handlebars and my heart doing a kind of flip-flop. Balboa had seen me.

"Hello!" a man's voice answered. "Looks like you took quite a spin!"

She'd been calling to the driver. She hadn't seen me.

And before that could change, I slipped my feet into the toe clips and tore onto the road.

I dialed the service station about an hour later.

"Lemkin Auto. Jonathan speaking."

I cleared my throat. "My name is Carol Balboa. My mother is Beverly Balboa, and I'm calling to check on her car."

"I just spoke with your mother a little while ago. What's the problem?"

Oops. "She's still a little confused. You know, the accident threw her. So if you don't mind telling me what you told her about how it happened . . ."

"Of course not." He sounded so sympathetic that I felt bad trying to put this over on him. "Somebody was messing around with that car. That kind of thing won't happen unless someone makes it happen. Wheels don't go sliding off axles every day. Your mother got any enemies?"

This was not good. I knew just what Neil would say. "Who's always messing around with cars? Von Findlay."

And it was even worse because, ever since the fire, I doubted that Judy and Corey were in on it. Before then, I thought Judy was the bad influence on Tony. But now it looked like it might be the other way around.

But maybe Donny knew enough about cars to do that kind of thing if Musgrove asked him to.

That's what I would've said to Neil if he'd been there.

The phone rang, and I hoped it wasn't Neil. Arguing with him in my head was one thing, but I didn't feel up to it for real.

"I got your message, sweetie. What's happening?" Art.

"Nothing. Everything. I don't know."

"You don't sound happy."

"I'm not."

"Want to tell me about it?"

I didn't know where to begin, but everything was such a mess, it didn't matter. I started with Mom. "It's this guy, John Ely, this sleaze who's been coming over and telling Mom she should repaint the place, and she does everything he says. It's making me sick."

"The paint?"

"Not the paint. That guy and the way Mom listens to him." I asked Art if anyone tells him how to fix his house.

"As a matter of fact, yes. A friend named Peter. He's got a good eye." Whoever Peter was, I was sure he was nothing like John Ely with his tan and his suits and his sicko sleazo way of talking. "What else, Carterkid? The case?"

I told him what I had on Musgrove. He started to laugh.

"What's so funny?" I asked.

"I was thinking I should be writing this down. I could get a show out of it. I'd call it 'The Case of the Unprincipled Principal.'"

"But the title would give it away."

"Only if he turns out to be the real culprit," he said. "Are there loose ends? Clues that don't seem to fit?"

"A few," I said, and explained. I also told him about Von Findlay, but I played it down.

"I don't know how to advise you," he said. "Taking on the principal could be a dangerous thing."

"I think I'm already in as much trouble with him as I can be. You can't get in much more trouble than being expelled. And if I can get enough proof to get Balboa to believe me, I won't have to worry as much about him."

"That's true."

"But if I *do* get expelled, can I move out there with you?"

Instead of an answer, I heard the click that meant Art was getting a call on another line.

"Carterkid, I've got to take this call. Get back to me soon and let me know how it's going." Then he was gone.

If I had the power, there are two things I would uninvent: nuclear bombs and the click that interrupts your phone calls like that.

There was an envelope addressed to me on the kitchen table. The return address was Thomas A. Dooley High School, Office of the Principal. Inside was a yellow notice: my hearing was scheduled for a week from Saturday.

I was sitting there trying to decide whether to ball it up and chuck it into the trash, tear it to shreds, or take the trouble to burn it, when I heard Adrian and Justin heading for the kitchen.

"I'm starting to get nervous. Opening night is coming up fast," Adrian was saying when she and Justin walked in.

"Carter, what happened to you?" Justin said.

"What do you mean?"

"You look like you just learned you have ten minutes to live."

I didn't think that was funny. I wouldn't have thought *anything* was funny right then. But especially not them. Their hanging on to each other, being so lovey-dovey all the time was getting on my nerves.

"What's the matter?" Adrian asked. "Case going badly?"

"What case?" Justin said.

Adrian had forgotten; Justin wasn't supposed to know about it.

I fixed a look on Adrian, and on Justin. Then I left.

"She must be in one of her moods," Justin said, opening the refrigerator. If Adrian said anything, I didn't hear it. I had gone to my room and closed the door.

The private investigator was closing in on the crook in the novel I was reading when Adrian showed at my room. I wanted to tell her to get lost, but I'd already been rude enough.

"Sorry to bother you," she said. "I just wanted to remind you about the meeting tomorrow morning."

"I forgot to tell you," I said. "I'm grounded on weekends."

"I know, but I talked to your mom and she said she'll let you out for this."

I shrugged and said I'd go. But nothing seemed to matter anymore. My hearing was coming up and I wasn't anywhere near prepared to prove my case — unless I came up with something solid on Musgrove, or discovered Tony was guilty and decided to risk losing him forever by getting him into the worst trouble of his life.

One thing was sure. It was going to be tough to get clues when I had to stay locked in all weekend.

Must be a love note from Neil. That's what I thought when I went for my bike the next morning and saw the piece of paper taped to my handlebars. He leaves them all the time. Sometimes he makes them up himself and sometimes he borrows poems from Shakespeare.

But this was no love poem:

"STAY ALIVE: STAY OUT OF IT. Ambassadors of Doom."

Like the note they'd sent to Adrian, the words were cut from a magazine.

I looked around; I felt like someone was watching me. If the threat was serious, how would they do it? Would someone hide under my bed and jump out with a knife? Or would I be cornered at school, strangled, and chucked into Musgrove's dumpster?

I didn't have to wait long to find out.

I was on a downhill, the kind of hill I'd normally take at full speed. But this one had a stop sign at the bottom, and taking it like that could mean coasting straight into a crash.

I squeezed the brakes to slow for the stop. The bike picked up speed. I squeezed harder. Still, I went faster. By the time I knew my brakes were gone, I was hurtling for the intersection.

I was going too fast to brake with my feet. Instead, I prayed no car would meet me down below.

There was no car. But there *was* a pile of gravel.

My tires hit, spun, and slid out from under me. The last thing I felt as I skidded along the pavement was the tiny black stones grinding into my skin.

"Justin, Justin, Justin." It was the only word I could remember.

"What's she saying?" It was a man's voice, real close, but real soft.

"Someone's name, I think." Another voice, even closer. "Honey, who's Justin?"

I tried to find the answer, but there was nothing in my head, nothing but the name. I confessed, "I don't know."

"What's your name? Where do you live?" I shook my head. Honestly, I don't know. Please guys, just let me sleep.

But no. They lifted me from the ground and into the back of a van. While they carried me I felt I was floating. It wasn't until the van door slammed that I realized what was going on.

"You're the paramedics!" I said, as if we'd been playing a guessing game.

"That's right. Now, hold tight. We'll be at the hospital in no time." I don't remember any faces, only voices. My thoughts were like furniture in a ship in rough waters — sliding all over the place. And then they were gone completely.

The next thing I was aware of was my head, and of how I wanted to get rid of it. The furniture wasn't sliding around anymore — it was being hacked to pieces with a sledgehammer.

I forced an eye open to see where I was. Mistake. Everything was spinning like some carnival ride. My stomach couldn't take those rides, and it couldn't take this either.

Where was a doctor or a nurse, anyway?

Then I was moving. Someone was pushing me from behind; the feel of the wheels underneath me reminded me of riding in a grocery cart when I was a kid. "Where am I going?" I didn't dare open my eyes again.

A woman's voice, husky, answered. "We're taking you to have your head examined."

"A lot of people would say it's about time," I said.

Next, two big guys slid me up a ramp into a monster machine. I felt like one of those pizzas I'd seen back at Pedroni's. "This is a CAT scanner," somebody said from somewhere. "It can see if there's brain damage."

You don't need that machine to tell you I've got brain damage. Anyone stupid enough to get mixed up in what I've been doing lately has *got* to be wrong in the head.

It was dark in there, and the *whir* of the machine didn't help any.

When they finally slid me out, an orderly wheeled me back into the emergency room, where this doctor straight out of a soap opera — young, big white teeth, nice haircut — put ten stitches in my head. If I hadn't been in so much pain, I would have been in love. As for what it was like to get stitches, I'd rather not get into that.

Justin and Mom were waiting. The hospital had figured out who I was by finding my school I.D. card in my purse. The card doesn't have my address or phone number on it, so I guess they had to call every Colborn in the greater Philadelphia area to find out which was missing a kid named Carter.

Mom had her hands up to her face, and was peeking through her fingers the way I do whenever a murder is about to take place in a movie. Slowly, she dropped her hands. "You look fine! I was sure you'd be a bloody mess."

"My head doesn't feel too good. . . . I landed right here." I pointed, but Mom didn't look.

"That oughta teach you to ride with no brakes," Justin said.

"How do you know about the brakes?"

"I picked up your bike. The brake cable was loose. Useless."

"I don't get it, how it could have happened," I said, forgetting for the moment about the note. It wasn't until I changed into a hospital gown and the note fell out of my pocket that I remembered.

The CAT results came back saying I was perfectly normal. "You're sure you're not keeping anything from me," Mom asked the doctor.

"We wouldn't do that." The doctor was a thin, pale woman, the exact opposite of the soap opera type who'd put in my stitches. "We're keeping her overnight for observation. It's standard procedure for head injuries."

"I just hope I have the full picture," Mom said.

"You hear so much about the shenanigans that go on in hospitals these days."

The doctor gave her a look that wasn't exactly sympathetic, and left.

"Is there anything you want from home?" Mom asked, getting ready to go.

"Merry. Please have her come. As soon as she can."

"Look at you, silly girl," Merry said, coming into my room. "In the lap of luxury. How'dya pull it off?"

"Mer, I'm glad you came. Look." I held out the note. "It was taped to my handlebars," I said. "And then I had the accident. Someone loosened the brake cable."

Merry just stared at me for a few moments, then tried to talk, but couldn't quite get anything out. I think she was more shocked by what had happened to me than I was.

"Who would do that to you?" she said finally. "Who could be that horrible?"

"I don't know. The note's my only clue."

"But there's not even any handwriting to go on."

"You could still trace it."

"How?"

"You could look through some magazines and find the ones that use this typeface — this shape and style of letters," I said. "Then you could try to find the issue that used these words in its headlines. Then you'd have to find out who gets the magazine.

"Will you do it?"

"I suppose I could . . ." She wasn't thrilled. Understandably. It could take a year.

"If you don't find anything, okay. But it'd be great if you'd try."

"Okay. I'll be back if I find something."

"I owe you forever."

She smiled as if she agreed, but couldn't quite say it while I was laid up like that.

"They're beautiful," I said to Justin, who was standing in the doorway with a bouquet of sweet william. "Thank you." He came in and bent to kiss me on the cheek.

"Neil said he's working on an excuse so he can get over here later," he said. "Looks like you've got more flowers coming." He pointed to the doorway, where a candy striper had parked her cart.

"I hope it's not because they think it's my funeral."

The candy striper lifted two arrangements off the cart and brought them in, blabbering away. "You must be one popular —" She stopped short when she saw me. "Carter!"

It was Linsey.

"They just give me a room number; they don't tell me who's in it." She looked me up and down, trying to assess the damage. "I heard about your accident. No fun. We missed you at the meeting this morning."

While she was talking, I noticed two other candy stripers at the cart in the hall. It took me a few seconds to realize I knew them, too. It was the pink-and-white uniform that threw me. These girls usually wore black.

Judy and Corey.

Justin picked the card off one of the arrangements. " 'For my darling detective, your devoted Watson.' "

"That must be from Neil," I said. "Who sent that one?" I pointed to the other arrangement.

" 'For my Carterkid,' " he read, " 'my perennial blossom. They won't keep you down.' " Art.

"If I ever landed in here I'd get poison ivy from my brother, and that would be it," Linsey said.

"Is that Judy and Corey out there?" I asked.

"Unfortunately, yes."

"I didn't think they were the type to go in for volunteering."

"They're not." Linsey was as disgusted by them as I'd been at the mall. "They got caught shoplifting a couple of months ago and the judge said he wouldn't lock them up if they did some kind of community service. So here they are."

"How long have you been working here?"

"About a week. Since I became an Ambassador. When do they let you out?"

"Tomorrow morning."

"That soon? So fast?"

"I'm only here for observation. There's nothing wrong with me."

"Oops." She checked her watch. "Gotta get moving." She started for the door. "Maybe I'll see you later. Sometimes I stick around to deliver dinner."

As soon as she left, Justin grabbed the remote control and switched on the TV perched on a shelf above my bed.

"Look at you," Adrian called from the door-way, holding an enormous bouquet and watching us watching MTV.

"Hi!" Justin stood and waved her in.

"Don't you know that stuff turns your brain to mush?" she said.

"It can't hurt us. After my accident, my brain is mush. And Justin's brain has been mush since birth."

"Good point." Adrian was talking to me, but looking and smiling at him.

I asked her about the meeting for the Ambas-sador–drama club dinner. "Everyone was sorry you weren't there. And they were especially sorry for the *reason* you weren't there. You'll still make the dinner, tomorrow night? And," she said, presenting me with the bouquet, "this is from all of us."

"I should make it. They let me out tomorrow."

"Oh, good," she said. "Here, let me find a vase for those."

Adrian found a container that could pass for a vase and moved Art's arrangement from my bed-side table to make room for hers. Then she gave me a tiny envelope — the kind you get at the flo-rist — with my name printed on it. The card said, "Get well soon! Love, Adrian."

"Thanks," I said, putting it next to the vase.

Then Linsey was back with a dinner menu and

a cartful of magazines. She gave the menu to me.

"Check what you want for dinner, and help yourself to a magazine," she said.

"I'm not hungry," I said. I was still too woozy to trust my stomach with food.

"You have to eat something," Justin said, looking the menu over. Adrian sat on the bed beside me, picking through the magazines.

"How about scrambled eggs, dry toast, and orange juice?"

"I don't care, Just. I don't think I can eat anything."

"You should at least try," Adrian said, pulling a *Mademoiselle* from the pile. "I almost brought you mine from home." She gave me the magazine. "It's got some great clothes."

Justin checked off eggs and gave the menu back to Linsey, who reminded us that visiting hours would be up in five minutes.

Adrian checked her watch. "I've got to go, anyway. *Dress* rehearsal." She took my hand and squeezed it. Then she squeezed Justin's, and winked at him. She and Linsey left together while Justin hung back to talk to me.

"I guess Neil didn't come up with anything good enough," he said.

"Spoke too soon." It was Neil, standing in the doorway.

Justin got up to go. "See ya tomorrow."

"So, what did you tell your mother?" I asked Neil when he sat next to me.

"The truth," he said. "I convinced her you

couldn't get me in much trouble while you were flat on your back."

"Thanks for the flowers."

"I brought you something else, although I don't know how useful they'll be in here." He reached into his pocket.

"Swim goggles? Riding boots?"

He handed me a packet of photographs. The close-ups of the snake in the elevator.

"Thanks," I said. "You're right. I don't know what I can do with them until I'm out of here. And even then . . . now they're leaving notes without handwriting — just words cut from magazines."

"Well." He got up and shifted from one foot to the other. "They said visiting hours were up, so . . ."

Oh no. He was going to kiss me. Please. Don't do this. But I could see he wasn't going to stop on his own. I started to cough, hard. And then Linsey came back. She told him it was time for him to scram, and handed me my supper tray. Neil smiled, backed away, and left.

"Maybe you shouldn't have much if you're not up to it," she said. "You don't have to eat any of this if you don't want to."

She stood next to me, ready to pull the tray away.

"Are you in a rush?" I said. "If you have to be somewhere, you can leave it. I can get a nurse or someone to clear it when I'm done."

"No, I'll wait. You probably don't want that much of it anyway."

She was right. The eggs looked like globs of yellow oatmeal. I shoveled one of the globs into my mouth and swallowed without chewing. It oozed down my throat and landed like slime in my stomach. I did it once more, then dropped my fork.

"Done," I said, already regretting it.

"Okay," Linsey said, gripping the tray and pulling it away. "I'm getting off in a few minutes, so if you need anything else, better let me know."

I dozed off for a while, and when I woke up a few hours later it was because a nurse was shaking my arm. "Sorry to wake you, but we always do this when there's been a head injury. The doctor wants to make sure you can become alert."

"That's all right," I mumbled.

"Is there anything I can get for you?"

I shook my head, slowly, because the sledgehammers were back, whacking at my brain. I leaned back to read my magazine, but my vision was still foggy, and the words spun out of focus.

I dropped the magazine on the floor, which might have been the ceiling for all I knew. I felt like I was spinning in a dryer with the heat on high. But I wasn't drying out; I was soaked through with sweat. I had never felt so sick in my life.

A new doctor came in with news the next morning. This one was short with pudgy fingers and a flat face that looked dirty around the chin, which was covered with dark stubble. The news he had wasn't much prettier than he was.

He said I had salmonella poisoning. "It usually comes from food that's been infected with the salmonella bacteria. It can also come from unsanitary habits, such as eating immediately after you've used the toilet, without washing your hands."

I didn't care where it came from. I just wanted to know when I'd stop feeling like someone was smothering me with an electric blanket.

"It'll take about a day for the worst to pass, but you'll be weak for a few days after that. We're going to keep you here today. Tomorrow we'll see about sending you home.

"You gave us quite a scare," he added. "It's not common to have only one case of salmonella poisoning. Once it gets into the food supply, it usually spreads like crazy. We expected half the patients to be sick with it this morning. But you're the only one."

"Do I get a prize?" My tongue felt like sandpaper.

He smiled and left me alone.

By the time Merry showed that afternoon I felt a little better. On the temperature scale, I was midtropical jungle rather than pits of hell. Merry was smiling, and her cheeriness made me jealous. I wanted some of it.

But then she saw something on the floor and her smile died.

It had been a long time since I'd seen Merry pissed off. She was then.

"You found it!" she said.

"What do you mean?"

"The magazine!" She bent to pick the *Mademoiselle* off the floor where I'd dropped it.

"What?" My fever had burned away any memory I'd had of the meaning of the magazine.

"The words. The words in the note came from this issue of *Mademoiselle*!"

It all came back like a boomerang. "No, I didn't know that. I wasn't even thinking about it . . ."

She smiled again, and sat on the edge of the bed to show me how each word in the note matched a headline in the *Mademoiselle*. I was still cooking with fever, but I got a chill seeing that note again.

"See? It's perfect," she said, pointing out how the word *stay* in the note matched the *stay* in the headline over an article called "Stay in Shape: Fitness on the Run."

The *alive* came from a story called "Look Alive: New Life for Old Clothes," and on it went, until it hit me like a snowball between the eyes. I knew who it was.

"Hand me that packet, please," I said, pointing to the photos Neil had brought. "And that." I pointed to something else on my bedside table.

I looked both over carefully, then pulled my legs out from under the covers. The backs of my legs were soaking wet. I slid off the bed onto my feet. The floor felt like a tippy canoe, not just because I'd been in bed for a day and a half, but because my discovery threw me off balance. I tried to steady myself and made for the closet.

"What are you doing?" Merry said.

"Checking out."

"You can't just—"

"I know who it is."

"Who?"

I told her and her hand flew to her mouth.

"And if I'm going to do anything about it, I've got to get to school right now."

"But you're still sick."

"I'd rather be sick a few extra days and enrolled at TAD, than fine when they ship me off to boarding school."

She got my point. "But how will you get out?"

"We'll just walk out. How many people can tell the difference between a patient and a visitor once the patient chucks her hospital gown?"

"Carter—"

But I was already dressed. "Please check the hallway."

Merry stuck her head out the door. "Uh-oh," she said. "Nurse on the way. And you're dressed!"

I ducked into the bathroom, leaving Merry to manage.

"Carter, what am I going to say?"

"Where's the patient?" The nurse got there before I could answer.

"She using the bathroom."

"Is she all right?"

"Oh, yes. She's fine. Fine."

It wasn't until she knocked on the door that I realized I hadn't locked it. While her hand was on one side rapping, mine was twisting the bolt into place.

"Are you all right in there?" She rattled the knob.

"Yes, I'm fine, fine."

"Okay. I'm coming on duty now, so if there's anything you need, let me know."

"Great. Thanks."

"Visiting hours are up in five minutes," she said to Merry. Her parting words.

Once we were safe in the elevator, we giggled like five-year-olds, all the way down.

The elevator doors opened to the front lobby and a view of Tony Von Thelan dozing in the waiting room. It didn't help settle my stomach any.

"What's *he* doing here?" Merry stopped to stare at him slumped over in his chair.

"Probably waiting for Judy to get off duty." I kept walking.

"Why don't you go say something to him?"

"What would I say? 'Waiting for Judy? How nice!' Besides in about an hour, we're going to solve this case. And I'd rather have that than Tony, any day."

"Bull," Merry said, covering her mouth as soon as she did.

When we got to school, Josh was hanging special lights so the cafeteria would look a little better than it does at lunch every day, and Linsey was dabbing the last bit of paint onto a banner welcoming the faculty. Bob Earle was slicing mushrooms and Adrian was at the stove, stirring.

Everyone was surprised to see me. You'd think I was a ghost.

Adrian was the first to greet me. "You sure you're all right? You still look pale."

"I'm fine. Just haven't gotten much sun," I said. "What can I do to help?"

"Look around and pitch in wherever you want."

A paper bag next to her fell over, and the top layer of carrot peels, onion skins, and orange rinds spilled onto the floor. I grabbed the bag, shoved the garbage back into it, and, hugging the putrid package, signaled for Merry to follow me out back to the dumpster.

"This is gross," she said while I picked through the garbage. "You really think there's a clue in there?"

"Believe me," I said, tossing junk into the dumpster, "I'm not doing this to find a new perfume formula."

"I wish you'd tell me what we're looking for."

"I want to surprise you."

"If you tell me, I promise I'll still be surprised."

"Yeah, right," I said. "Loves me," I said, tossing a tomato paste can into the dumpster. "Loves me not." I chucked a frozen spinach box. "Loves me . . ."

"Carter, you are nuts," Merry reminded me.

I shrugged and continued until the bag was empty.

The clue I was looking for wasn't there.

*   *   *

Musgrove was in the kitchen when we went back inside, standing over a cutting board chopping an onion.

"We're doing the work for you tonight," Adrian said, holding out her hand for the knife.

"Cooking's not work," Musgrove said. "It's always been a hobby for me. But," he said, turning over the knife, "whatever you say, boss."

"You can go out into the cafeteria and wait for dinner to be served. It won't be long."

"Yes, ma'am," he said, and left.

"So, what next, Sherlock?"

I had no idea.

Not until Adrian gave me one.

"Carter, I just thought of something you could do for me," she said. "I have to get something from my purse, but I left it in my locker. Would you watch the stove while I get it?"

While Adrian was gone, I gave Merry some instructions.

"I can't believe what you're asking me to do," she said.

"Please. I promise I'll never ask you to do anything again."

"Oh, *sure*."

"Please. I mean it."

Merry shrugged. She'd do it.

Adrian came back with her bag.

"Can I see your purse?" Merry said, springing into action. "I've been looking for one just like it."

"Sure," Adrian said, handing her the bag.

Merry unzipped it. "Just want to see the compartments. Looks pretty roomy." Then she turned it over to look at the bottom. Everything emptied onto the floor.

Everything. Including the clue I'd been looking for.

"I'm sorry!" Merry said. "Let me help you."

"No!" Adrian bent to scoop the contents back into the bag. "I'll get it."

I pulled Merry aside to give her more instructions.

"You promised you wouldn't ask any more favors."

"This is part of the *same* favor," I said. "Just go to Musgrove. Tell him what we saw in her purse. Tell him who we suspect, and make sure he knows *you* suspect the same person, because he'd never go along if he thinks it's just my idea."

"Okay, but you come with me."

We walked over to Musgrove, who was spearing a cherry tomato with a toothpick and dunking it into onion dip. Merry nudged me to talk first.

"We can trap the person who's been after Mrs. Balboa," I said.

Musgrove believed me as much as I believed in the tooth fairy. He ate the tomato.

"She can prove it, Mr. Musgrove," Merry said.

He was listening now, because Merry was talking, not me. He even kept listening once I took over. I told him who it was, how I knew, and how I planned to prove it. But by the time I finished explaining, he wasn't listening anymore.

"With your imagination, Carter," he said, "surely you could come up with something better than that." He speared another tomato. "Either make yourself useful around here or go home."

We walked away; talking to him was pointless.

"Blew it," I said. "I knew he'd never believe me."

But what if he was faking? What if he was in it after all?

"You think he's part of it?" Merry couldn't swallow that. You'd have to do a lot to convince her that a teacher, any teacher, would do something wrong.

"Why else would he ignore everything we had to say?"

"You're not exactly the most reliable person," she said, explaining how he might see things. "Let's go home."

"Are you nuts? You saw the evidence. Balboa's going to get hurt unless we *do* something."

She agreed and waited for me to come up with the something we would do.

"Would you please carry some stuff out to the table?" Adrian called to us.

I took a platter of rolls and Merry brought two water pitchers. Almost all the teachers were there, dressed up and looking nothing like their everyday selves. Mrs. Morris the gym teacher was even wearing makeup. So was Balboa. She looked pretty good, but unless I could get someone to do what Musgrove had refused to, she was going to look awful by the time she got through dinner.

Then I saw someone who'd do it. Or might: Justin.

I told him what I wanted.

"Why? What's going on?"

"I can't go into it now. Just do it, please?"

He shrugged, and agreed.

A few minutes later, everyone was sitting with their soup in front of them. But before anyone started, Musgrove stood and clinked a spoon against his glass.

"I have an announcement," he said. "Some good news and some bad news. The good news is, I have a new job. The bad news is that the job is not at TAD."

Everyone looked at each other. Surprised.

Musgrove went on. "I've just bought Pedroni Pizza. I'm leaving TAD to become owner and chef."

That explained the time he spent at Pedroni's — in the back business office, the one place I hadn't looked.

And it meant he wasn't competing with Balboa. So he'd have no reason to send anyone after her.

When the applause died down, Justin stood. "Congratulations, Mr. Musgrove." Then he looked at me, and I held my breath. "I know this dinner is meant to honor the faculty, but I'd like to invite Adrian to join us, to thank her for the work she's put into planning the evening."

The teachers clapped, and called for Adrian. With one exception. Balboa didn't look pleased.

I pulled a spare chair to the table, to a space

next to Balboa. Then I slid Balboa's soup bowl over. "I'll get you another — just a moment," I said to Balboa, while she looked at me with her mouth open. In seconds, I was back with Balboa's soup, and Adrian was turning white, then red, trying to refuse the invitation. "Thank you," Adrian said. "But I can't. I have to supervise, and then I have to get into makeup."

"Just for the first course," Mrs. Rogers said.

"Thank you," Adrian replied, looking away. "But, really, I have too much to do."

"Baloney," Musgrove said. "You have a capable staff. Now please. Join us. We won't take no for an answer."

"Okay," Adrian said, going slowly toward the seat. Then, as she sat, she let her elbow catch the rim of her bowl. The soup was gone, all over her shoes.

"She must be nervous about the play," I heard someone say.

But that wasn't it.

Merry bent over the spilled soup, not with a washrag, but with a drinking glass, which she used to scoop up some of it.

"What are you doing?" Adrian said.

"Collecting a sample," I said. "We want to show Mrs. Balboa your secret ingredient."

"What are you talking about?" Adrian was bright red.

"This," I said, reaching into her shoulder bag.

"That's my purse!" she said.

"I know. And this is yours, too." I held up the clue that had spilled out of the bag earlier. A petri dish. Full of salmonella bacteria.

Adrian was breathing so hard I thought she'd faint. Instead, she tore off, leaving everyone with their mouths open, and Justin with his head in his hands.

The show did not go on that night. Or any other night.

CHAPTER 13

I was supposed to go first, but Neil was already there when I showed for my hearing. It was going to be in the conference room behind the office, where I'd been twice before, each time so my teachers could tell Mom how disappointed they were in me and how they were sure I could do much better if only I'd apply myself more.

"You ready for this?" Neil tried to sound casual, but his voice was all over the place.

"Yup." I felt so guilty for making him go through it, I couldn't look him in the eye.

Mrs. Balboa stuck her head out the door. Musgrove couldn't even wait until the end of the year to leave TAD, so she was already principal. "Carter, we're ready."

There were ten people around the table, looking as serious as you'd expect considering what they were there for. I was dressed to make a good impression. Otherwise, you'd never catch me in a gray pleated skirt. I sat in the one empty chair at the table, between a woman I recognized as Wayne Davis's mother and a man I'd never seen before. Skinny, pale, with huge glasses, he looked like how I imagine Neil would as a grown-up.

"Carter," Mrs. Balboa said, "we're here to decide if what you've done — breaking into the student files and cheating on your biology exam — justifies expelling you from TAD. Do you have anything to say before we start?" She looked blank. Even after I'd saved her life.

"Yes," I said. "First, I'd like to thank you for giving me this opportunity to defend myself." That opening wasn't my idea. It was Art's. He said I should sound as humble as possible.

"Second," I said, "I would like to admit that I did trespass in the principal's office, and it was wrong." Then I did something else Art had suggested. I looked a few of the committee members right in the eye. That was to assure them I was being honest, and to make them feel I was trusting them with my fate.

"Then why did you do it, Carter?" Mrs. Davis said.

"I wanted to discover who was trying to hurt Mrs. Balboa. I thought the grades might be clues." I glanced at Mrs. Balboa. She still looked blank. "Now I know I went about it the wrong way." I saw several smiles. Points.

"And about the biology test," I said, reaching

into my bag for my tape recorder. "I have something here that will explain it." I put it on the table. "The first voice you hear will be mine. The other is Linsey Curtis."

I switched it on.

"How did that cheat sheet get on my books?"

"I put it there."

"Why?"

"Because Adrian Attridge threatened me."

"What did she threaten you with?"

"She said she'd tell about something I'd done."

"And what was that?"

"I painted the snake in the elevator so it would be there when Josh locked her inside it. I brought my paints from my art class. Only I didn't know what Josh was going to do. I didn't find out until after."

"How did she get you to paint the snake?"

"She said it was an initiation rite — for the Ambassadors. We were supposed to play a few pranks on Balboa. She didn't tell us they'd get so serious, or that we'd have to do stuff to you, too."

I looked at Balboa again. She wasn't bored anymore.

"Why me?"

"She wanted you kicked out so you couldn't investigate. And when that didn't work, she wanted you hurt."

I switched Linsey off. And this time when I looked at Balboa, she looked away. I could understand. It's hard to admit you're wrong.

No one said a word. They just looked at each

other like that was the most incredible thing they had ever heard.

My strategy was working. They didn't care about the rules I'd broken anymore. They wanted to hear about the Ambassadors.

"First," I said, "if you want to understand what's been going on around here, you have to know about Adrian Attridge."

I said Adrian was insecure. "She needed to feel she was controlling people. So when she became head Ambassador, she used it to get people to do things for her. And she did it in a very sneaky way. She convinced them they were playing harmless pranks on Mrs. Balboa as initiation rites, then used those pranks against them to get them to do more dangerous things, things that might scare Mrs. Balboa into leaving the school."

I knew from watching the lawyers on Art's shows that the best way to make a point is to ask yourself a question, then answer it.

"What did Adrian have against Mrs. Balboa? The fact that Mrs. Balboa knew she was a phony. Adrian could get by her other teachers with smiles and clever conversation. Mrs. Balboa was onto her. And Adrian couldn't stand it. She wanted everyone to think she was perfect. But she wasn't even doing her own biology project. My brother practically did it for her.

"Now you want to know what kind of proof I have, besides Linsey's confession," I said, wishing Art could see me. Then I went through my list:

Bob Earle put the pornographic pictures into

Balboa's lesson book. Adrian then used that against him to make him steal Mrs. Balboa's car keys. Then she used *that* against him to get him to start the fire in the lab, and finally to wreck the axle on the car.

"She had extra influence over Bob Earle, because he was in love with her."

She got Josh to make threatening phone calls, then used that to get him to wire the transparency projector for the shock, then used that to get him to lock Mrs. Balboa in the elevator. "I should have figured the elevator out a long time ago," I said. "The drama club had play practice the night Mrs. Balboa was locked in. So Josh, Linsey, and Adrian were at TAD when it happened."

That left two incidents that didn't fit. One was the frog in Balboa's lunch. That happened *before* Adrian became head Ambassador. The other was the glycerin in the closet, which happened on the day she won.

I had asked Judy and Corey, and gotten them to admit to the frog. "And Adrian poured the glycerin on the floor herself. She was mad at Mrs. Balboa for refusing the flower she offered her and making fun of her in front of everyone."

A man across from me was shaking his head. "I'm sorry," he said, "but I find this impossible to believe. Why would anyone, especially good students, go along with something like this?"

"*Because* they are good students," I said. "They have perfect records. Adrian gave them a chance to 'let loose,' with the pranks, which still seemed pretty tame. Then she threatened to tell about the pranks unless they did something worse, and they were willing to go along so they could keep their records clean. Each of them had a shot at a good college, and Adrian knew how important that was to them. She knew because it was that way for her, too. Getting into a good school was all that mattered . . . it mattered more than a biology teacher," I said, looking at Balboa.

"How on earth did you figure this out?" the man next to me asked.

I told him I was tipped off by four things that happened while I was at the hospital.

First, Adrian told me the Ambassadors missed me at their meeting Saturday morning — and that they were sorry about the *reason* I had missed the meeting. But they couldn't have known what that reason was, because even my own family didn't know I had had an accident until Saturday *afternoon*, hours after the meeting was over. The only way they could have known about the accident was if they'd caused it.

Second, at the hospital Adrian gave me some flowers and a card, then Neil brought me the photographs he'd taken of the graffiti in the elevator. The printing of my name on Adrian's envelope and the printing of the words "Balboa Beware" in the elevator looked like they could have been done by the same person. The little curlicues on the ends of the *a*'s, *e*'s, and *r*'s in "Carter" and "Beware" made the lettering look almost identical. And almost is as close as you can get when you have one set of words printed on paper and another on an elevator wall.

Third, the words in the note on my bike were cut from the issue of *Mademoiselle* that Adrian said she had at home.

And last, I was the only person in the hospital to get salmonella poisoning; someone probably put it in my food. Justin was teaching Adrian how to culture bacteria, so she knew how to grow salmonella. She brought it with her when she visited me, and got Linsey to scrape it into my eggs. Just like she did with Balboa's soup. I described how nervous Linsey was when she brought my dinner, and how she was practically warning me against eating it.

"Before Adrian tried to hurt me, she tried to throw me off," I said. "She showed me a threatening note she said someone had sent to her. She was convincing, too." I reached into my bag again, this time for a vial of clear liquid. I stuck my finger into it, then dabbed the inside corner of each eye. "She came to me in tears," I said, making sure every one of them saw the glycerin tears on my face. "She used glycerin, which she also used to make Mrs. Balboa slip on the floor.

"She decided to try to hurt me right after I caught her with Bob Earle. She thought I'd overheard her convincing him to mess with the axle." She invited me to the meeting and the dinner to placate me, I explained, but she planned to make sure I'd never get to them. When she came to the hospital and saw that I might get out in time to attend the dinner, she slipped me the salmonella."

That was it. I was done.

The room was quiet for a moment; then they

turned to each other and whispered what sounded like their amazement.

"Before I make a recommendation to the committee," Balboa said, smiling so she looked like the kind of person I could be proud to have rescued, "I want to thank Carter for her persistence in solving this case." She looked, smiling still, straight at me. Then, unfortunately, she went on. "Yet I suggest you concentrate on the fact that she *did* break into the office computer. If an adult were convicted of this charge, he or she would face a ten-year sentence in the penitentiary."

So much for my strategy.

Then she asked me to leave, warning me not to talk to Neil while I waited.

Neil and I sat across from each other, giggling. It felt ridiculous.

Finally, she called me back.

I sat again and Mrs. Davis turned toward me to give me the news. "Carter, we've decided to let you stay at TAD. However, you are barred from participation in extracurricular activities and membership in school societies."

In other words, there goes my newspaper career.

"Do you have anything to say before we dismiss you?" Balboa asked.

There was plenty I *wanted* to say — about how Balboa might show a little gratitude, and how pointless punishment was on top of my knowing that what I'd done was wrong. But it would only have gotten me into more trouble. So I kept it short.

"Please don't punish Neil," I said. "He was just going along because I begged him. He didn't want to do it."

Some of them nodded. But that could mean anything.

Now it was my turn to wish Neil good luck. I was about to, when he said, "I have something to tell you. A confession."

"Okay . . ."

"I found out what Judy was doing at Von Thelan's house." He looked down. "She takes private art lessons from Tony's mother."

I'd never told him about the time I'd seen Judy at Tony's. Merry must have been the one.

"And the reason he was at the hospital was to wait for Peter, who needed a new cast."

Merry, again.

There was nothing to say, so I did it. Kissed him. But not on the lips. Way over on the cheek. Then I ran outside, where Justin was waiting to take me home.

CHAPTER 14

Justin looked the way I would have looked if I had been expelled.

"Everything's cool, Just," I said, sliding in next to him. And it was true. Of course, the punishment made me mad. But at least I could stay at TAD. And Tony wasn't with Judy. I had a chance.

He nodded like it was old news, and turned on the ignition.

"Are you going to tell me what's wrong, or do I get to tickle it out of you?"

"Nothing's wrong."

"And I am the Queen of Rumania."

"I feel like a jerk, that's all."

"About Adrian?" He nodded. "You're not the only one who fell for her bit. You shouldn't take it so hard."

"I even *knew* she was using me . . . but . . ."

"I know. You liked her and you hoped it would turn into something."

He nodded. "I'm such a jerk."

"You are not a jerk for wanting to trust her. *She's* the jerk for being someone who can't be trusted!"

He nodded again. "I wonder what's going to happen to her."

"You mean when she gets out of the mental ward?"

"It's called the Care Unit," he said.

"Whatever . . ."

"I mean the rest of her life."

I shrugged.

"And what about the others?"

"Being suspended for the rest of the year isn't going to impress too many colleges."

"It *will* impress them . . . not in the right way," he said.

"You know what still gets me?"

"What's that?"

"Musgrove letting Donny off so easy all the time."

"Donny's never broken into the computer," Justin said. "What you did was worse than disrupting class or picking a fight."

"I know," I said. "But I can still get pissed off about it."

"Mom's got a few people at the house," he said, changing the subject.

"Like who?"

"I only recognized one of them. They came while I was pulling out. The one I recognized was that real estate guy."

"That sleaze," I said. "Do you think he and Mom . . ."

"I don't know." He didn't like the idea any more than I did.

When we got home, the visitors were gone.

"Oh good. You're here." Mom walked in behind us, holding a cigarette. "How'd it go?"

"I can stay," I said.

"Good," she said. Not "Great" or "Whoopee!," or "Terrific." Just "Good."

"Now, sit down. I have something to tell you."

Uh-oh. Same words she'd used when she told us she and Art were splitting up. Same words she always used to tell us something she knew we wouldn't want to hear.

"Just because I haven't mentioned this to you before doesn't mean I haven't given it a lot of thought. I have." She lit the cigarette and tossed the match into a clay ashtray I'd made in first grade. It was a mold of my handprint.

"I've put the house up for sale," she said. "We're going to move. I've found a place in Havertown."

The phone rang. Mom went to get it. Meanwhile, I sat there wondering what the chances were that this was all a big joke.

"It's for you." She waved the receiver at me. I couldn't stand to look at her just then, so I went to take it in the kitchen.

"Hello?"

"Life at hard labor." It was Neil.

"What?"

"That's what they gave me. Life at hard labor."

"Very funny."

"What's wrong?"

"I'll put it this way. I might as well have been expelled."

"What?"

"We're moving."

"*What?*"

"I can't talk now. First I have to find out if this is for real. I'll call you later."

"Okay . . . and Carter?"

"Yeah?"

"They let me off with a warning . . . about hanging out with you."

I hung up and dialed Art. "The thing that kills me," I said, "is that I should have seen it coming. I went and solved this huge mystery at school, and meanwhile I had no idea what was going on in my own house."

"What were the clues?"

"There was this guy snooping around at Mom's party, this realtor. Then he started coming over and making suggestions for fixing up the place. Justin and I thought he was Mom's new boyfriend. But when she went out with him, she was looking for a new house. And when they were here, they were fixing our house up for the market. I should have at least *suspected*.

"Also, Mom's been complaining about how hard it is to take care of the house, and how much she hates half the people in town — even though she invites them all to her stupid parties —"

"Go easy, Carter. . . . Your mother may not have done the right thing by keeping it a secret from you, but, listen . . ."

That's when he invited me to California for the summer.

And what happened next is another story and a half.